Peter Anderson is a forensic psychiatrist and a member of the New South Wales Police Medical Board. He lives in Sydney with his family. Golf Interrupted is his first novella.

Golf Interrupted

Peter Anderson

First published by Peter Wallace Anderson in 2017
This edition published in 2017 by Peter Anderson

Golf Interrupted

EPUB format: 9781925579468
Print on Demand format: 9781925579475

Cover design by Red Tally Studios

Publishing services provided by Critical Mass
www.critmassconsulting.com

Contents

Contents

Prologue

Sebastian had first met Donnie more than ten years ago. She had no feathers.

He'd been around to visit Noel in his cave below the fourteenth tee at Desolation Point. The cave was special, with its views over the reef and rock islands, but on that day there was something far more special for Sebastian to see.

Sebastian had sweated on the clever hermit for the fifteen years since his breakdown. Lizzie from the surf club had found Noel hanging from the communication tower beside the lifesavers' radio room. He was blue, but because Lizzie was qualified in resuscitation, Noel almost came good again. She had the rescue helicopter on the pad within minutes and Noel was taken to the emergency department at

St Bernard's. From there it was the psych ward, and it had fallen to Sebastian to supervise his friend's failure to return completely to the realm of alleged reality.

Sebastian remembered his first meeting with Donnie like it was yesterday. "Who's this?" he'd asked Noel, when he was confronted with a great sea-going bird who had lost all her feathers. "It's Donnie," said Noel, swivelling to look at Sebastian with his one good eye. "She likes Donnatella pears. That's why I call her Donnie." Donnie was indeed eating a pear in a corner of the entrance to Noel's cave. She was up against the heater, from which a long extension cord ran all the way to the lifesavers' complex with its helicopter pad and radio room. Lizzie had come to trust Noel once again, and provided electricity along with the use of the facilities. In return Noel would fill in a radio shift when they were short. His local knowledge was invaluable.

When released from hospital, Noel had taken to making sculptures of birds, from the moving parts he salvaged by night from the local kerbside clean-ups. He used sensors and computer parts to put together a sculpture of a great sea-going bird. "It's responsive to wind," he said, pointing to the sensor, then to the wingspan on his model. "When I'm finished, you'll see the wing tilt in response to the wind. Say, a three club wind from the north-east, you'll see a fifteen degree tilt into the wind."

Noel no longer had many needs. Once he'd needed to be club champion, and when that was not enough, it was the British Open. He approached his holy grail like a chainsaw approaches soft wood. He qualified from Desolation Point but on the second day of competition, he was blown away by a real wind coming in off the Irish Sea. Then it was downhill. He was a golfing casualty. After the hanging he did not know why he'd done it.

"It was the three minutes without oxygen before you got to him," Sebastian told Lizzie. "He's lost some vision and his recent memories. It's a blessing. Otherwise he might do it again."

Lizzie said that Noel had been saved by a pelican. "It would have been forever if that pelican hadn't raised the alarm."

Sebastian was unsure whether it was failure in his suicide attempt or the brain damage that had fixed Noel up. In any event, Noel underwent a transformation. He almost forgot about golf, although in the club's bar they told stories about Noel with his eye patch, coming out when the weather was really bad and there was no-one on the links. "Trying for redemption after falling off the cliff in bad weather in The Open at Hoylake," they said. Some others said he was a mirage, or a ghost, but Sebastian and Lizzie knew the story.

Sebastian had put him on the pension and because Noel would not go out in normal weather, did his banking and Centrelink forms when required. Noel was accumulating wealth – his outgoings being limited and the full pension coming in. He started sponsoring artists, mostly sculptors, as long as they were close to nature. "It's the beauty that keeps us going," he often said. Lizzie helped keep him clean and he seemed to have come to terms with his life as he ascended into a mystic fascination with birds.

Sebastian sat with Noel on that day, as he did most weeks after his round of golf. And he watched Donnie closely. She was very quiet and accepting. "She didn't know what hit her," said Noel. "She was crazy to be out on the links in the lightning. She stumbled down the cliff path out of the storm, and here she is. She can't fly, she can't feed herself. I thought she was done for but she's coming good. I've finished with all those other bird sculptures," he said, "now it's pelicans for me."

Months passed. Noel brought in the fish and Donnie got stronger. The feathers grew back and her departure was imminent. Donnie waited for Sebastian's weekly visit. As soon as he arrived she nodded her great bill in farewell, then ran for the cave mouth, flapped her huge wings and lifted skywards. The day was calm but there was an updraft that took her above the cliffs.

"Where's she going?" asked Sebastian.

"They go back to where they've come from," said Noel. "Let's watch and we'll find out where that is."

Donnie wheeled northwards, then westwards over Desolation Cove, then she glided down and onto the light tower between the first tee and the eighteenth green of Desolation Point Golf Links.

"There you are," said Noel, "back to the golf links. Like you and me. I hope she stays out of trouble, and comes back to me safely when there's lightning."

* * *

When the gentle one came, I was soon glad. The other one, with the eye patch, stopped pacing and muttering. When that one became still, he spoke softly - of the ocean and the breakers on the reef, of the cliffs and the clouds. All the while he shared the warmth of his fire. He said he liked flying and his eyes lit up. I knew then I could trust him. He said he'd flown when younger and I knew he was the special one.

There had been the flash and I was lost. I didn't know where I was and then I was in the cave. I could see, and he was the one, the one I found hanging off the great tower. Sebastian called him Noel.

Sebastian was the one who touched me. "Hello Donnie," he said. "Pleased to meet you, I'm Sebastian." Then he went away and came back with his bag and out came the oil, olive oil he said, and he poured it over every inch of me, and massaged. He came back every day. I couldn't leave the cave.

When Noel went fishing I was alone. I could see some of the others flying past the cave entrance but they didn't know I was there. I moved up from the pears to the fish but still I was weak for a long time. I didn't like the needles but I let Sebastian do it.

Noel nursed me through. I'll never forget him. He watched over me as my feathers grew back. When I grew strong, I leapt from the mouth of the cave and I could fly.

I settled back on my little tower, over where the golfers come. The other pelicans didn't want to know me. It was the scars, and I'd gone over - to the other side.

I resumed my fishing, and I kept my watch.

1

The nightmare again. His chest was wide open and his heart quivered in the grip of a masked assassin. His blood flowed red, in a fly-over of needles and tubes, distant from his body.

Sebastian woke with a start. He sat on the edge of the bed and checked for a pulse – fast and irregular. He had refused the pacemaker. "Are you suicidal or just crazy?" the cardiologist had asked, yet he lived.

While Magda slept on, he rummaged in his bedside drawer for his pills. Noises.

He got himself up to check. There was an altercation outside in the street. Better than having the head noises within. The time? 3 a.m. Day? Tuesday. Thank God, the appointment with the wretched cardiologist is not until tomorrow. "Your last chance," the doctor had said. Today he was free. He didn't have to attend the mental hospital and he would not carry a phone. He couldn't face news of another death. He'd go to golf. He longed for the sound of the wind and waves, and prayed there would be no surprises to interrupt his game.

He needed the bathroom and, as usual, checked his face in the mirror above the handbasin – he couldn't help himself. The nose was still not straight and the ears were still not matching, the tops bleached by the sun. He must find a hat. The teeth were uneven, but they worked well. *This is the face you've got, make the best of it.*

But he kept checking it, all the way to the cancer scar under the eye. The skin had looked nasty again and been biopsied. He didn't want to know the result.

He got in the shower and directed the hot water over the scars of the coronary bypass surgery and all the other operations. He loosened up. He massaged the scarring of the childhood burning, gave thanks and reminded himself that his wounds gave him strength. Then he counted last week's golf shots, the number of drives that found the fairway, the greens reached in the regulation number of strokes, the number of pars, birdies, bogies. He reviewed and counted the excellent shots and the appalling shots. The excellent shots were always to do with the wind. He would move the ball left to right into a right to left breeze so as to keep it straight. He would draw it right to left into a left to right breeze, holding a line against the wind. He would then go high to hitch onto a friendly zephyr or go low under a headwind.

There was always something to be learned in the counting, as the soothing water cascaded and the ageing body rejigged itself. He had told his golf partner Stefan that he counted, and Stefan said he preferred to spend his time out of the shower and actually practising. The Rabbi, his other partner, had just shrugged. Sebastian cherished his golf partners because mostly, in professional life, he operated alone.

He counted pelicans too. He focused on Donnie, his favourite pelican, but sometimes when the breezes were right and when the fishermen pulled in to Desolation Cove, there were scores of fat pelicans. He liked to estimate how high Donnie flew on the thermals. She was very good at catching an updraft by the cliffs and riding it to the top, soaring above Desolation Point, then gliding back to her light tower. Her flight could all take an hour but he knew that Donnie could stay aloft for twenty-four hours at full wing stretch, over the wild ocean if necessary. He reported to himself in terms of the height she reached – a thousand metres today, five hundred metres another day.

He was a keen observer of pelican social behaviour. He had seen Donnie fishing with mates when the tide was low, circling in the shallows together, herding fish into a tighter and tighter circle, flapping and paddling until the noose was drawn, then scooping the fish into the pouch, swivelling, positioning, and swallowing the catch. Donnie's diet was exclusively fish. She was on top of the food chain, much like he was.

When she flew, she flew alone. And on her electric light tower overseeing the windblown links, she was solitary. The other pelicans took little notice of Sebastian, but Donnie seemed obsessed, watching, following him, and demonstrating for him the subtle wind shifts by her flight. She was drawn to him. Like Sebastian, she was a damaged loner.

* * *

My scar is stronger than what was there before but I'm not the same. When you meet someone else who's been broken, there is a special vibe. Noel now, he gets it. Noel does not have many connections. I can see he's frightened. But he's got me, and Sebastian, and Lizzie, and Hugh the barman. I don't get around like I used to do, but Noel – he doesn't get around at all. He says he's OK because he's got me, and the ducks and the rabbits, and he's got the beauty. Sometimes he sounds OK. But sometimes he mutters - about the golf and the people coming – and I don't feel right about him.

From my tower I watch. Sebastian comes every week, always at dawn. He lifts his nose and he points himself into the breeze and sniffs. He doesn't wear a hat and he shakes his hair so it gets blown in the wind. Then he checks that I'm here on my tower. He looks and he nods. I nod too and lift my wings to say hello.

2

To pass the time before dawn, Sebastian read by his desk lamp – the coroner's brief about the fatal police siege at Landsborough. He was glad he had not seen this gruesome death and was merely the expert reviewer. As a forensic psychiatrist he often dealt with the very mad and the very bad. He worried about another siege and he thought another death would take him down.

He failed to concentrate on the brief so he turned his attention to a book gathering dust on a shelf. It was written by his friend Stefan, a professor of philosophy at the University of Sydney: *The Suicidal Jihadi: an indifference to life*.

Sebastian was disturbed by the title and turned away. He was troubled by his friend's interest in suicide, and preferred to think of him as a C-grade golfer lifting himself towards B-grade.

He started to read the police file on Zak, a jihadi returned from Syria and now incarcerated at Callan Park Mental Hospital. The file contained ASIO reports but they were heavily redacted. He had lived in Baghdad until 2007 and was just 8 years old when the family fled to Syria, along with more than one million Iraqi refugees. There was the flight to Indonesia, the delay, the boat to Christmas Island. A skeletal account was there, but there was no personal story. Refugee status was gained. The United Nations definition of refugee was satisfied because his father carried a well-founded fear of persecution based upon religion. The family were settled in Sydney when Zak was 12 years of age.

Zak had been returned to Australia by the police in Turkey, but he had been detained on the way out of Syria, not on the way into that country. The documents were full of self-congratulation about new partnerships with Turkey and the building of intelligence sharing relationships. None of this had been redacted.

The Australian legal papers however were clear. He was imprisoned and charged upon return to Australia. But he was not convicted.

Sebastian tried again to read between the lines of the redacted documents which told him as little as

Zak himself was prepared to divulge. Again he failed and again his mind drifted. A year ago, Sebastian had been lured to the re-opening of Callan Park, which had closed fifteen years earlier.

He had stood among the sandstone buildings and the green lawns, which rolled ambitiously to the rock walls that held back the tides and transformed the mangrove swamps into cultured and precise borders. The landscaping was an attempt to contain the uncontainable. There had been no expense spared in those golden days of nineteenth century enlightenment. The mental hospital had become unfashionable but now was back with renewed purpose.

"Sebastian, there is a brink, and we're on it."

He paused and looked hard at Superintendent Jones. When she first broached the possibility of him resuming his work at Callan Park, Sebastian was incredulous. "There is evil at the gate," she said, "a death cult." Whatever did she mean? She had always been like this. Dramatic. And then she would get around to what she meant and what she wanted.

"Sebastian, we want you to tell us what we're to do with these returned jihadis."

The super wore the routine sort of undercover garb she used to wear in the drug days: jeans and sneakers, beanie and dark glasses. She moved with Sebastian across the lawn outside the School of Arts, where there were angry art students attempting a sit-in. They had been evicted to make way for terrorists. Sebastian remembered the building as the old Ward Two, the high security unit for the criminally insane.

Jones gestured at the crumbling sandstone façade and then at Sebastian. His mind went to the fire in Ward Two – an insane murderer had set fire to his mattress. Sebastian had to intubate the man to keep him alive, while the firefighters did their work around him. Again he saw the blackened walls and the ghostly handprints groping for the locked door. Sebastian too had seen the merits of burning the place down but later, when he was in charge, he turned it around and the hospital found its moral compass.

"Here's the capacity to accommodate them, and everything locks adequately enough, yet the liberals can't call it jail," Jones continued. "We've got a hundred jihadis lined up for you, Sebastian. Which ones are evil?"

Something in Sebastian went off at the word *evil*. "I don't know anyone who's evil," he said. "The more I understand them, the less evil they are."

"These jihadis are not all mentally ill, Sebastian," said Jones. "Some are just bad."

"What I know is that there are weak people, or sick people. I don't even call them bad – unless I've a very good reason."

"OK," said Jones. "We have a hundred jihadis who have been through the courts and not convicted.

We need to know which ones are just plain nutters. Who can be released into the community with the usual surveillance? On control orders? Electronic monitoring?"

Jones had grabbed him at the elbow and steered him away from a small group of women in full black dress, with niqab. "Let's get over here a bit. They're not necessarily just visitors – possibly miked up." And she went on to recount her own experiences wearing the full black in south-western Sydney shopping centres, cafes, and mosques, miked up and gathering what intelligence she could for the Counter Terrorism unit. She paused beneath a watchful magnolia and observed a group milling around the building that had housed the NSW Writers Centre, now commandeered by ASIO and Federal Police. "What's your thinking?" she asked.

"It's funny," he said. "They wanted to shut the loony bin, and now they want to open it. They used to want me to discharge all the loonies and now they'll want me to keep them. I can't just lock them all up Jones, just because you can't convict them. I'll treat them as people."

"Of course," said Jones.

"And it may be a life and death decision about who's allowed to go, just like in the old days." Sebastian recalled that his intubated murderer had made a recovery, later escaped and murdered again – a drinker at the nearby Garryowen Hotel. "I have to be very sane to make these big calls. I'm not sure I am."

"You know these things. We don't know. We just say 'he's mad' and don't want to know the rest – it's too disturbing. We think you know what goes on beyond that line where we sign off. We think very highly of you, Sebastian."

"I'm working on it," he said, and she looked at him. "Hard to get much from my colleagues. My best mate suggested a bullet to the back of the head, and he's a philosopher. I told him I didn't think that was right. And he said, 'Well, who are you working for?' Who would I be working for, Jones? The jihadi, you, or some politician?"

"No problem there," she said. "Clearly, it's a confusion that would trouble only an amateur. You could handle it, you're used to having wild ones arrive with a police officer on each limb, or even on court orders as an alternative to something more dire."

"You're like a bloody politician. You didn't answer my question."

"You're a healer." Jones knew this was Sebastian's weak spot. In his dream he was a healer of broken minds and spirits, and once this dream had been bigger than life.

Later on, Sebastian felt he had been talked into his new role assessing jihadis just as easily as he'd been talked into his old role helping police at sieges. At the time, however, he'd viewed it as a new chance. Psychiatry wasn't on the way out after all. It was just changing. "Some of them are victims – just traumatised kids," he'd said to Jones. "A bit like you when you were doing that undercover work. And you're not evil. How old were you? Twenty-five or so? All ambition."

"That was me," said Jones. "You helped me, I was getting traumatised."

"But not permanently damaged," he said.

Sebastian's mind returned to the police file on Zak. The jury did not convict – the prosecution had gone for too much, witnesses recanted and some were deemed unreliable. Did he remain a danger, asked the police, or could he be released? Sebastian remained troubled by Zak – a disturbed childhood in a war zone. He'd begun to talk, a little. Just how scarred was he? The worst thing was the holy war around his head. His father was Jewish, his mother Muslim, and the Baghdad community didn't like that. He had become a refugee and Sebastian had more sympathy for that. Then a stint as a jihadi in the Caliphate, with an undisclosed series of atrocities, and he was only seventeen. *How do we really know what he did?* Was he just a victim, or did he remain a jihadi?

Sebastian also remained disturbed by Zak's beautiful older sister Leah, with the auburn hair and bluish eyes. Yesterday she had pressured Sebastian to release her brother. He had refused. *I can't cope with another crazy death.* Her anger was disturbing. Sebastian's mind began to drift over sieges, dead bodies and terrorist bombs. He didn't know the answers and he didn't want another death.

Time passed slowly, it was still early. He dressed slowly. The radio reported deaths so he turned it off. Then he planted a kiss upon the sleeping Magda. "I remain alive and I'm hoping to be back," he whispered. "I love you."

He packed an organic banana – the extra potassium being good for cramps. He checked once more his bracelet: *Not For Resuscitation.* He went out into the first light.

* * *

As the first light fell crimson on Desolation Point, Noel Davies struggled barefoot up the steep path from the rock platform to his cave. He carried a fishing rod in his right hand and in his left, a billy can. Only one fish in it, but soon the sun would come over the ocean horizon and he would be revealed. He was vigilant as usual for the lone pelican as she descended in wide spirals from a thousand metres. The ragged and once handsome man met the still handsome pelican at the mouth of his cave.

"Good morning, Donnie," he said, and the old pelican raised herself up to her full height and extended her wings to reveal the scarring beneath. She flapped gently. "Only one fish," he continued, as he tossed it towards her magnificent beak. She caught the fish easily, pointed her beak to the crimson sky and swallowed.

"No breakfast for me again," Noel said, as Donnie nodded then turned to face her ocean and her day, "but you're the one with the work to do. One more time, Donnie. Sebastian will be coming."

Donnie jumped from the edge, flapped powerfully and laboured briefly before soaring on the updraft as Noel watched her with his good eye and smiled.

* * *

Across town in the Eastern Suburbs, Sebastian's golf partner made hurried preparation. The Rabbi obligingly ate his miserable diet breakfast, something delivered to the door after subscribing to an expensive plan. Esther was watching closely but he had secreted several chocolate bars in his shorts for later. Golf required energy and he felt depleted. He'd been late to bed because he was writing a eulogy for another Holocaust survivor. He felt a burden, carrying the weight of the Holocaust, but knew that today's golf would lift him.

"I hope that Sebastian fellow doesn't make you miserable again today," said Esther.

"I do worry about him," said the Rabbi.

"Well don't. The point of the golf is to play golf, and keep yourself fit for the grandchildren. I don't know why you golfers have to bear the weight of the world."

"He's my friend," said the Rabbi.

"Have you looked in the mirror lately?" asked Esther, as she noted the stain on the Rabbi's favourite golf shirt.

"I need this shirt," he said. "I'm superstitious."

"And who's Leah?" she asked.

"Poor Leah," said the Rabbi. "What about her?"

"She rang last night when you were late at the synagogue."

"She's a quandary," said the Rabbi. "Lovely girl. It's very hard to explain. She wants to join the faith but her mother was Muslim, and her brother's a jihadi."

"What?" said Esther.

"It's too hard."

"She sounded desperate."

"I'll catch up with her later," called the Rabbi as he headed for the door.

"Don't forget you have a funeral at four," called Esther as he disappeared. "Another of your Holocaust survivors. You can do it. Have you got your suit?"

"Thou shalt not kill," whispered the Rabbi, and then chided himself. "You've got to stop saying that."

* * *

From my tower I see a lot of golfers. I remember faces. Some have the same face all the time. Some have changing faces, like the bald one. I have to know when a predator is coming. I watch.

When the wind blows my flying is easy. It's the stillness in the air that I hate. But these golfers curse the wind.

Sebastian likes the wind. When it blows he has his head up and he laughs. He's always looking at me. I try to help. I show him by pointing into the teeth of it and I show him where I can glide and bank with the wind ruffling under my wings. He takes from his bag one stick and looks at me, and then he puts the first one away and takes out another stick to hit the ball.

3

Running fingers through his thinning wavy hair, Sebastian stood by the teeing ground and faced the sea breeze as it crossed the reef and dunes, then funnelled into the green and through the scattered ranks of early morning golfers.

A two club wind ruffles the minds of golfers. When the pelicans soar in this wind, and when the boys on hang-gliders soar above the point, the mind can soar also, with dreams of dancing, at one with the wind, giving in to it, using the wind to advantage, perhaps fighting and defeating it, bending the ball into its teeth, to make it straight and nullify the wind. When it lifts to a three club wind, the older pelicans retire and watch from their lifesavers' radio towers, as the mad golfers try to fly.

The breeze bristled past the building labelled Desolation Point Surf Rescue. Sebastian imagined Lizzie with her knitting and her binoculars, settling down by her radio for a long shift. The breeze swerved at the cliff face along from the Surf Rescue and Sebastian pictured his childhood friend who had cheated death and now dwelt in the cliff caves. Did he get breakfast today? There would be a chance to check on Noel later.

Sebastian liked to go uncapped to allow the wind to have its way in his hair and in his head. He had come to know the wind, as much as it was knowable. *Yes, I am coming alive again.*

Stefan came up behind him. "I can't find my balls," he complained, as he fiddled with the car keys, the glasses, the wallet, the scorecard, the glove – it was all in a mess. "And if I don't make B-grade today, that's it. I'm killing myself." Stefan was facially expressive, and his golf entailed a full facial workout. Lines around his eyes and mouth came and went. His eyes inclined to the bulge. He had all his teeth, except for the back molars whose extraction he had described to Sebastian in minute detail. Stefan could not stop talking when he ate on the golf links, and this drew attention to his teeth. Sebastian could see the fillings and crowns in his mouth, in which Stefan had reluctantly invested much of his money.

Stefan swung his clubs with such gusto that he was not predictable. The technique varied with subtleties of mood and demeanour. After he had swung, his pleasure or displeasure was immediate. His perplexity over the result then followed. Why was a professor of philosophy engaged in seemingly banal activity? The rest of the week, he was in his head, thinking about his important topics and lecturing on death, suicide, terrorism and euthanasia. At golf, he scratched his chin, furrowed his brow and wrinkled his nose. He shrugged, he slumped and he stamped, as he wondered in his head if he was good enough.

"Would you like to use these balls?" suggested Sebastian, hesitant about giving in to the professor's suicidal threats.

"I got mine from Aldi," said Stefan. "Best deal, and now I can't find them."

Stefan was jumpy today, quick in his movements and thoughts. He wore his wide-brimmed white hat held down with a band under his chin, baggy white shorts, white ankle socks, black golf shoes and a long-sleeved blue business shirt buttoned at the wrist.

"Hope this hat stays on," he said. "I am concerned about the sun damage. I've had the freeze-off six times. I'm destined for cancer. You know what Jenny said when I left? That I looked like someone in the Famous Five stepping out for an adventure. I've got the bald spot too. Can't play without a head covering, it's fatal."

Stefan was distracted by the sight of black cockatoos wheeling off towards the dunes. They flew with a touch of implausibility, like fully laden Wellington bombers taking off from a field in Yorkshire, just clearing the fence and the cows. Stefan loved their flight as a sign of hope. He felt inspired that he too would defy the odds and progress into B-grade.

"Are you OK?" asked Sebastian.

"Yeah. Jenny doesn't know I'm suicidal. And as long as I've got suicide to fall back on, I can get through."

Sebastian, hoping to avoid violent death, felt strangely reassured. Then he spotted the Rabbi emerging from the clubhouse locker room, where he had hung up his black suit to be worn later at the funeral. His baggy King Gee shorts were fastened with a smart leather belt, which made them bunch and give the appearance of what children call Harry High Pants. The Rabbi rubbed hard at his jaw.

Sebastian had spent much of his waking life looking at faces, and he considered that the Rabbi had a kind face, if a little worried. It was intelligent, curious but unlined and unmarked, the complexion soft. The Rabbi's hair was incomplete but also soft, the missing bits were covered by his golf cap. Sebastian knew that at other times those missing bits were covered by a skullcap or a formal black hat. The Rabbi looked as though he had not seen the sun, even when he came in from the midday sun after the golf. He was a little pudgy. Always the food was an issue, especially the chocolate bars, which had given him a toothache today. He had dropped some weight recently, because he was in competition with his brother. That was why his shorts were baggy and his belt drawn in an extra notch. He moved very well for a pudgy sixty year old, but never excessively. He was contained, he did not engage in the big swing, just as he did not engage in hyperbole. He smiled and laughed but did not double over in mirth nor lose himself in sorrow. He was reliable in his demeanour, his outlook, his dress and his golf. Sebastian took in his predictable appearance and was comforted.

"It's a three club wind," said the Rabbi, in his BBC English.

"I wish it was, but isn't that an overestimate?" asked Sebastian, still measuring the breeze through his hair.

"No, it's not," said the Rabbi, "the wind is moving the beard." He stroked his lush black beard to reinforce the point. "The beard's the relevant test of a three club wind. No good for you tallish people," he said to Sebastian, "it will disturb your centre of gravity. For us short fatties, it's not so bad." He patted his tummy. "Anyway I'm opening with the two iron, not the five, it's a three club wind."

Sebastian knew that just as one could not safely predict the weather in the mountains, so the seaside golfer was stretched to know what the wind would do next. He had his old woolly jumper in his bag, the one knitted by his mother. He was kitted out as usual. He found this the best approach – to follow routine. He had his golf outfit, just as he had his mental hospital outfit for Thursday, and his other doctor's outfit for Friday, with the red tie, not the blue. Now it was the striped t-shirt and the older blue shorts. No glove. He did not believe in the glove, and it pleased him to be a bit disreputable. He told himself, "It's not important enough to spend the money, and I'll get another few wears out of these outfits."

"Who's our fourth today?" Sebastian asked the Rabbi. They did not have a regular fourth player and Sebastian wondered about this. He speculated that most golfers found the trio unusual and elected not to play with them.

"I don't know," said the Rabbi.

"Me, I'm with you. Brian here, Brian the dentist," came the gentle reply, like an Irish rain moving in over Connemara and settling down for the winter.

Sebastian turned to greet the tall and smiling figure approaching them. He was pleased. He felt saner when Brian was there and wished it were more often. Could it be that Brian could not take their company every week?

Brian had graduated from Trinity to work long days on the wide-open Irish mouth – poor dental hygiene, too many sweeties, and a bit of the malnutrition. So he had chosen Australia. There was no future in Ireland, he told his mother. Her aunt had gone to London and grand-aunt to New York, saying something just like that.

"Good to see you, Brian. You know, I wanted to be a dentist like you," said Sebastian, "but I was dyslexic and I enrolled in Mental instead of Dental. I graduated a psychiatrist and got all those troubles. I know bugger-all about teeth."

Brian, who tolerated almost anything, just smiled.

The four men stood close together on the first tee. It was their time. All looked happy now, and each carried hope.

Sebastian was to hit first. The first hole was known as *Hope*, and this name was printed on the scorecard and engraved upon the metal plate bolted to the sandstone that marked the teeing ground.

Donnie, in her place on the tower, was pointing fifteen degrees east of due south. Sebastian had noted Donnie's retreat to the tower, and then her more detailed guidance. He took the four iron to keep the ball low under the southerly, and struck it on a course fifteen degrees east of south. The drive came around nicely in the wind and as he turned in acknowledgment, the old pelican raised herself up and flapped her wings in appreciation. Sebastian thought Donnie might have said, "Well played," but he was unsure.

"It's no fun inside the mouth, Sebastian, you're better off in the brain. I did have a good job, dentist at the Guinness factory, but I turned my back."

"I know it," said Sebastian. "I used to pass the factory every day when I worked in Dublin." And his mind tumbled along the cobblestones from the cathedral down through the Cornmarket past the betting shops and the Guinness factory, and turning into St Patrick's Hospital for the alcoholics where he did his time. "And what do you do now then?"

"I handle complaints for the Dental Association."

Sebastian tripped over a small tussock but kept himself nice and upright. "Complaints about dentists?" he enquired, thinking he may have misunderstood.

"I talk to the complainants," said Brian.

"You don't have to look in their mouths?"

"God no!"

Brian had the stride of a second row forward and Sebastian, with his arthritis and metal joints, struggled to remain abreast as he tacked into the fifteen knot wind. "What do you talk about?" he yelled into the teeth of it from a distance behind the bigger man.

"Teeth," replied Brian, stopping at his ball.

"All day?" asked Sebastian.

"Oh no, not all day." Brian selected his pitching wedge and targeted the first green. "It's not an Atlantic wind," he declared, "otherwise I'd be taking the five iron." Without fuss he stroked his ball, which arced handsomely.

"You're on the green," said Sebastian.

"I'd hope so," said Brian gently. "It is a minimal breeze after all. Now, about the teeth. I do find that after we've talked about the teeth there are other things to talk about, unless we get stuck on the teeth."

What fortune, thought Sebastian. He has the perfect job. He would talk anybody out of anything. He could coax the potatoes from the fields of Connemara.

"And I also identify dead bodies at the morgue –"

He was interrupted by some young women golfers coming up behind them. "Why don't you blokes get a move on, you're already slow!" one of them called.

Sebastian was used to this, because he limped, and because the women walked quickly. What has happened to civil society? Brian loomed larger than a legend and handled the matter. The callers shrank off.

"People aren't what they used to be," Sebastian heard himself say out loud, and had one of his visions of corpses, which had become alarmingly frequent of late. This one was a corpse at a police siege.

An old pelican came in low over Sebastian's head, flying from cliff to beach, aided by the fifteen knot wind. He thought it might be Donnie venturing out again. He wasn't sure. She didn't hover or circle as Donnie did, but went straight for the beach. Fisherman just in with a catch. Maybe Donnie had a better offer.

"Do you think that's Donnie?" asked Sebastian.

The Rabbi, perplexed, said, "Who's Donnie?" He rubbed his jaw. "This toothache's killing me."

Could the Rabbi be losing it, like from Alzheimer's? "The pelican," Sebastian shouted, and repeated, "Donnie the pelican." Why is it that he had to repeat himself for practically everybody – the old, the unintelligent, and now the Rabbi. *Perhaps we've played golf together too long.* Why didn't anybody know Donnie's name?

"I don't really know about pelicans," said the Rabbi, "but I do know that my granny, when she stopped rocking, always said that pelicans meant death."

Sebastian had not heard this before. He thought it superstition and became more concerned about the Rabbi. He made a mental note to speak to the Rabbi again so that his own funeral could be put in motion. He heard the soft whirring of a distant helicopter. It unsettled him, for the helicopter could mean death, a life saved, or an outcome somewhere between.

Sebastian drew the four iron to approach the green from 150 metres. He decided against the practice swing because there wasn't time to waste. He struck the ball sweetly. It soared but caught the false front of the green, then rolled back down the slope and finished twenty metres short of target.

"Bad luck," said the Rabbi, who had settled into his convivial and worldly self, putting aside for the time being all recollection of hate speech, discrimination and persecution – matters that had troubled him as recently as 5 a.m., while Esther slept soundly beside him.

"Do you call it luck?" asked Sebastian, starting to grind his teeth. "They make life hard for the old people," he said, addressing his remark towards a passing hang-glider, then again towards the disappearing Donnie, and then repeating it to the rescue helicopter descending from 200 metres for a high wind landing on the beach pad.

Lizzie leaned out and called to Sebastian over the rotor with exaggerated mouth movements and gesticulations. Normally she just patrolled and looked out for idiots in trouble. He waved back with no idea of what she wanted, but as the helicopter got nearer, he could see she was agitated.

Perhaps it was the Rabbi pulling on his arm but something stopped him in his relentless path towards the first green, where he felt a par could still be salvaged. As the helicopter descended further, Brian's ball was moved by the downdraft and rolled down the false front, just as Sebastian's had done. And as the helicopter landed on the green and Lizzie from the surf club emerged in her fetching green overalls, he saw that it was not Lizzie at all but an unidentified man in black, with bulletproof vest and gun holster. The helicopter was not the rescue helicopter, but was black. It bore the insignia of the New South Wales Police.

Sebastian reminded himself that he was due for his annual eye check. And he cursed the police and their emergencies. He refused to carry a cell phone but they knew his routine and where to retrieve him at 7.50 on a Tuesday morning. He felt his pulse – now very fast and what doctors call "irregularly irregular". He heard again the words of the cardiologist – "You're a time bomb." He felt for his bracelet and wondered if he should have accepted the pacemaker.

* * *

I don't like the big black bird. It's loud and it's fast and it takes Sebastian. I tried to follow but I was frightened and I was too slow. I don't like to go too far, since the scarring. Sebastian is inside the bird and I can see he doesn't want to be there. When Sebastian goes in the bird, Noel starts to mutter and pace up and down. I don't like that at all. I hope he doesn't go over by the great tower, where he was hanging, all that time ago.

4

As it flew north, the police helicopter was followed for a short time by a pelican. The helicopter pulled away, and the pelican banked to turn south.

Sebastian surveyed the coastline. The cliffs were forbidding, the boulders ragged, and the surf roiling. Some distance beyond Point Shipwreck, he did not recognise his location and he was lost.

He used to know himself. He could be relied upon, to bear the pains of life, like rosemary in a buttonhole. But not since the bypass surgery. He was a finely honed piece of machinery, with multiple tolerances and feedback loops of self-recognition. All gone now. He felt coarse, and when one thing went wrong, there was no recovery. Again his eyes went to the crashing surf.

When the helicopter landed on a grey football field, Sebastian was hustled by a man in black into a matching black vehicle. He dreaded all this. And visions of a corpse came quickly, for the second time that morning. Then he imagined the Rabbi getting a call on his cell phone by bereaved family – about the same corpse and its funeral.

Barely half an hour had passed since he was happy. He tried to get the emotion back by visualising the Rabbi playing his customary fade shot up the right-hand side of the short second hole. The image was blurry.

The black vehicle pulled up in the entrance way to the Paradise Motel. Chief Inspector Williams loomed large in dominant blue and opened the car door. "Doc, we need you."

Seventeen police sieges, counted Sebastian, and not a fatality on my watch. He knew the time was coming. *Why did I allow myself to be talked into this?* They know my routine. I don't even have privacy on the links.

"This is the poor rural version of Struggle Street, Doc. Two neighbours hate each other, one's been installing electronic surveillance to watch the other, who then fired arrows at the techies on the roof. I don't know why they were up there in the middle of the night. The techies called triple 0 and Bob's your uncle." Eyes on the uniform, Sebastian wondered what Bob Williams would look like in golf shorts.

"The SWAT team have set up a perimeter," Bob continued, "and they've evacuated the techies. Inside it's just the occupants of the one property, fortunately. I've been here since 4 a.m."

The clock in the foyer of the Paradise Motel showed the time as 8.20.

"Who's negotiating?" asked Sebastian, and was pleased to hear it was Sonia, whom he knew from training and from a previous siege. She was young and straightforward, with a reluctance to unleash the men in black. But nevertheless, she and they were a package.

"Who called for me?" asked Sebastian, as he took in the scene of the motel's foyer, transformed by ammunitions, vests, and electronic equipment. His eye kept coming back to rest on the brochures for the nearby Koala Park, visible just out the back of the motel and past the swimming pool.

"Sonia. She's down the road on the inner perimeter, where she's got visual contact with the property, and telephone contact with Matthews. We both have telephone contact."

"Who's Matthews?" asked Sebastian, as a large truck pulled up behind them in the driveway.

"Twenty-nine year old male, with a woman. He's known to us and to you guys, for overdoses, and he's been in the prison hospital. I've got two forensic psych reports."

Sebastian struggled to concentrate as men unloaded large lights, noisily, outside the motel's entrance.

"You expecting to be here after dark?" asked Sebastian.

"Yeah, and I've ordered in the meals too," replied Williams.

Williams was an older officer who Sebastian knew had lost his nerve, and had sensibly retreated to administrative ranks. He was the senior officer at the scene and therefore responsible, but he had delegated effectively when calling in SWAT. In reality, Sonia was in charge.

Wearing a bulletproof vest troubled Sebastian. It was compulsory – a precaution. "Procedure," said Williams.

"Better than being dead," said an officer in black passing behind Sebastian and carrying the largest gun he'd ever seen. Sebastian had a quick flash of himself on the slab, bulletproof vest and shorts, but he was untroubled this time. He substituted images of the Rabbi marching down the funnel of the third fairway, the dunes on the windward side, on the lee the little hillock where the starlings nested. Then the Rabbi was in his armchair with the grandchildren on his lap.

"One report says he's paranoid psychotic," came the voice of Williams, bringing Sebastian back to reality, "and the other says he has a personality disorder which flares up with 'ice'. What do you make of that? I've got twenty-three pages saying he's mad and twelve pages saying he's just a druggie. We need your interpretation, Doc. Tell us who we're talking to here…and how to talk to him."

Sebastian lacked confidence in Williams, who had once been his patient. The image of command and control had been blown, despite the overwhelming blue uniform. Williams had cried in the office and used up the Kleenex. The officer was now clueless at assessing risk, ever since the death of his mate Evans, an equally experienced officer. Evans had seen an opportunity, but he got it wrong. Williams was responsible on paper, so he was the one the hierarchy went to. The press crucified him. The coroner's inquest was still coming. "Such a common situation," he had said to Sebastian in the consulting room.

"What's your own information?" asked Sebastian.

"He's six months out. Nothing on our intelligence until the last two weeks. Then it's all neighbour complaints on both sides of the fence, uniformed officers attending more and more, advice given about apprehended violence orders. Nothing about weapons until shooting arrows at the techies in the night. The forensic reports tell you what he was like before the last six months. There's been no psychs since then. Coffee?"

How did all this happen? I was in a nice occupation helping people with family problems and that sort of thing. Then increasingly it was violent men, returned soldiers, police. The cases were all about death. Violent, crazy and unjust death. So much of it, he had felt half dead himself. One more could finish him off. Then a quiet word from a fellow psychiatrist. "Would you mind relieving me while I'm away," Richard had asked. "I do police sieges. It's really just supporting the police in their negotiations. Help them distinguish between the truly paranoid and the merely inadequate. You can do it on your ear. Sometimes you get these really inadequate guys who just want to be noticed. You can tell from their history, or by the way the negotiation goes. You give them a pizza and you're halfway to a solution. Maybe a bit of personal publicity will clinch it."

A Channel 7 truck parked in the driveway as Sebastian ran his eye over the paperwork. The heavier tome came from a colleague who made his living in the courts as a forensic psychiatrist. A quick glance was enough for Sebastian to know that the paranoid psychosis angle was a hopeful attempt at mitigation that had not succeeded. Matthews was probably not mentally ill at all. But these days, the ordinary battler was likely to have a diagnosis, even if it was a simple personality disorder. Even the police were more likely to have diagnoses, as much as they hated it. Their diagnoses were PTSD rather than personality disorder, but in the end there were similarities. Pulling a trigger was final. It didn't really matter if you thought you were attacked by extra-terrestrials or if you saw yourself in mortal danger from scumbags. If you pulled a trigger in error the result was the same.

"Well?" asked Williams. "What, Doc?"

Sebastian knew Williams as old fashioned when it came to psychiatric diagnosis. He had self-diagnosed "head noises", when he had to see Sebastian. He also diagnosed "the sadness". Both related to his friend being shot and killed. The head noises were the replays of his friend lying dead, then the death message to his missus, and then the constant thoughts, the what-ifs.

"He's sane," said Sebastian, "or he was sane when he last went to court."

"Good," said Williams. "If he sees the whole of New South Wales Police against him, he'd be correct rather than paranoid."

"I need Sonia now, to tell me exactly what he's talking about," said Sebastian. "Is he clean and sober?"

"Hello, Sebastian," came a woman's voice. His mind went momentarily blank. Most police people called him Doc. His name had baggage, the result of something deep in his mother or father, impenetrable even for someone who turned out a psychiatrist. And sometimes he believed that he would not have turned out this way if his mother had called him Pete or Jack. It could have been worse, he told himself by way of consolation. "Get over it," said his brother Tarquin, who preferred to be called Charlie. Sebastian had never met another Sebastian, but he knew that Saint Sebastian had been shot full of arrows, and then that the principal character in *Brideshead Revisited*, Sebastian Flight, had become hopelessly drunk on a regular basis.

"Sebastian," she repeated, and he then looked up from the report and saw Sonia in her black overalls, framed against the light coming through the mock-Corinthian entrance of the Paradise Motel. No, she hadn't put on a few kilos; it was the bulletproof vest.

"Hi," he said, "how's it going?"

"Oh fine, everyone's settled."

"I suppose they're pleased to have me."

"You know how it is. They always think it's worse when you're here. Not just an armed scumbag to deal with, but an armed scumbag with head noises. But I'm glad to have you."

Sonia Simpson had been a patient too, sensible enough to put her hand up after her first siege ended in a fatality. "I don't care if you put me off duty. I'm telling you how it is!" Williams, on the other hand, saw psych intervention as a bad career move and tried to second-guess the required answers. There is no right answer, Sebastian had told him. "Don't put me out, Doc. It'd kill me!" Williams said. He was probably right about that. *First do no harm,*

Sebastian reminded himself, the good doctor's guiding motto. Applying it was not simple. It would harm Williams to put him out of the force, but what about keeping him in the force? Everybody here was armed and dangerous.

"Why exactly did you want me today?" asked Sebastian.

She smiled. "I need to know whether to send in the pizza, and whether to give him anchovies."

This was once a private joke between Sebastian and his mentor Richard, who had enlisted Sebastian's help before relocating to Bermuda. The joke had been shared by Sebastian in the police negotiators' course of 2010, and he had since been defined by it. "What did the doc say? Do we send in the pizza or the men in black?"

Sebastian obliged her with a laugh.

"Seriously, Sebastian. What do you make of the psych reports? I couldn't get much."

Sebastian found the question disarming. "What my grandmother would have called twaddle," he said.

"I've never heard that expression," she said.

"And my mother would say it was tommy rot," he added.

With Sonia he felt life stirring. She reminded him of his first serious relationship, someone from the hospital, an athletic young physio who was as direct as he was oblique. The lovemaking started on the cricket pitch at the university number one oval, in the dark of course, and went out from there in spiral pattern through the med school, the library, the nurses' quarters, the overnight students' room, the physio gymnasium, and came to rest in the student share house down the road where it did Sebastian a lot of good, more so than the collected works of CG Jung, with which he had also been wrestling.

"I don't know that one either," she said, and Sebastian gripped hard on his senses, swallowed, and adjusted his tight bulletproof vest.

Behave yourself, she's half your age, she's a patient, and she's armed.

"Sonia, there's not a lot here that's helpful. He is, as your mates would say, a scumbag with head noises, but the head noises are pretty minor. Unless he's back on ice."

"He's not, his granny's been on the phone. And she's been watching him, up till now." Sonia's phone rang and she walked away, as the Channel 7 truck pulled out of the driveway.

"They used to stay where I put them," said Williams gruffly, as some rubbernecking tourists put their heads out of their motel rooms and were corrected by a large constable.

"That was Granny Matthews again," said Sonia. "She says her boy's arrived at her place."

Williams and Sebastian looked at each other.

"So who are we dealing with?" said Sebastian. "You've had me profiling this character Matthews from his medical records, and it's not him."

"Granny says he lets lots of his new student friends use the place," said Sonia, "so it could be any one of a number of them. He doesn't know who."

"Who said it was him in the first place?" demanded Williams, his face still blank.

"I told granny we'd be needing him to make an identification," said Sonia, "but he's gone out again. She doesn't know where he is. So for now, we don't know who we're dealing with."

Nobody said anything, but the silence was interrupted by the sounds of the police truck unloading twenty lunches at the front door of the Paradise Motel. These were to be delivered to a team of twelve men in black, currently taking cover behind sheds down the road. Also to the police negotiator, Sonia, who was hoping to get away in time for the pick-up from child care. Plus one psychiatrist adviser, who had missed breakfast altogether. Then there were Williams and his support command, most of who looked like very good eaters. It was 8.33 a.m.

"They come from central kitchens," said Williams. "We don't have to deal with McDonald's any more. It was so embarrassing."

"Any leftovers for the principals in there?" asked Sonia, gesturing down the road towards the location of the siege.

"Before we start feeding him, whoever he is, does he have demands?" asked Williams.

"He hasn't demanded anything really," said Sonia. "Sebastian thought we might solve it with pizza and a session on the Channel 7 news."

"Hang on," said Sebastian, "that was on the basis that he was sane, and that he didn't want suicide by cop. We don't know that now. He might be mad."

Sebastian turned to the technician by the large flat screen showing a still of a bare-chested man, multiple tattoos visible.

"Looks like a jihadi," said the technician.

"Whoa! What makes you say that?" said Sebastian.

Sebastian looked again. No, it wasn't Zak – this man was much older. He chastised himself for checking. *Surely they would have told me if there had been an escape.*

"He does look like a terrorist," said Williams. "I'd better brief Counter Terrorism."

"Bob, you're jumping the gun," said Sebastian. "You don't know this is terrorism."

Bob Williams shuffled and peered at the screen. "I'm not taking chances," he mumbled.

Oh no, that means Jones and she sees terrorism everywhere. I won't be able to restrain her. She'll go to full throttle and smash the joint, before she says hello.

"Can we get a close-up on those tatts?" said Sebastian. "See," he said, when the picture was enlarged. "See the left shoulder. It says 'Maccabiah Games, Tel Aviv, 1997'. But see, Bob, it's in English - and Hebrew. Can't be terrorism."

"I don't know, Doc, it looks dodgy. I'm supposed to think of terrorism."

Sebastian looked harder, trying to get past his aversion for the tatts. The man had Semitic or Arabic looks. He had Zak's athletic build and proud bearing. He hadn't taken much notice of Zak's tatts – he didn't like them, and anyway, the legal identification came through biometric mapping of the iris. *I should have looked closely at Zak's tatts, but no, this one is way too old.*

"Anything else?" asked Sebastian, giving up on the visuals and turning to Sonia.

"He's not saying anything else, he told me, until he gets food, sees himself on Channel 7, and has a conversation with a Rabbi, definitely not a psychiatrist. He might talk to Rabbi. Then he said something about golf but he mumbled. I couldn't get it."

"Know any Rabbis?" enquired Williams, of no one in particular.

"Don't you have a police Rabbi?" asked Sebastian.

"Yes, we do. And he's on the golf course."

<h1 style="text-align:center">5</h1>

Perhaps an hour had passed since the Rabbi was taken from the Desolation Point Golf Links and chauffeured by police helicopter. His passage was watched by a ragged man and a pelican standing in the mouth of a cliff cave below Point Desolation. The police helicopter quickly diminished to a speck as it flew north along a line of towering cliff falls.

Then the Rabbi had been taken by unmarked black vehicle to the epicentre of the siege. He had been pointed to the front door of a fibro premises with minimal briefing. His instincts told him not to enter the building, but he had fatalistically complied with police instruction and his own sense of duty. He had gone in.

The Rabbi trembled as he emerged alone from the fibro premises. "Thou shalt not kill," he said, and immediately chided himself. "You just don't have to say that." Then he mumbled, "How does a golfer turn killer?" and slapped his wrist.

A German shepherd sniffed him then sat alert at his feet. His handler, following protocol, asked the Rabbi if he was carrying anything and would he take off his golf cap and empty his pockets. He had a chocolate bar, a golf ball and a part-completed scorecard that showed him with a winning score at the fourth hole, where his round had been interrupted by the police helicopter coming to fetch him. The hole was known as *Danger*, and the Rabbi had previously linked that name with the water hazard that ran the length of the fairway on the right.

The dog, Schroder, was happy when the chocolate bar came out, but he gave the Rabbi a second run over. He had been imprinted on ballistics, gunshot and bomb residue as well as food items. Schroder resumed his at-ease position. Sanjay the dog handler did not relax for he knew there was more to come. He motioned the Rabbi to step away, and moments later he was grabbed by several men in black who appeared from behind an iron shed. Then the Rabbi was put in the black vehicle and taken for debriefing at operational headquarters, the nearby Paradise Motel.

The Channel 7 cameraman, walking backwards in front of him, filmed the Rabbi as he walked to the doorway of motel, not knowing whether to look solemn or confident in his golf cap. He wore the lucky polo shirt with the stain on the collar. He was more embarrassed when the camera panned down to his baggy shorts, then knees and then black socks, which were technically against club regulations at Desolation Point Golf Links.

Once inside he spotted Sebastian dwarfed between large men in blue and was pleased to see his friend. He knew Sebastian hated police sieges, but respected his friend's capacity to handle a crisis. He felt in good hands with Sebastian.

The clock in the foyer showed 10 a.m.

"Sebastian," said the Rabbi, "this fellow is tattooed, and we don't allow tattoos. On his face and back, he insisted on showing me. Maccabiah Games, Tel Aviv, 1997. It was the year people died when the bridge collapsed. I fell in the river with the rest of the golf team. He knows. It was awful."

"I remember," said Sebastian. "We had to play without you for two months."

Sebastian had never heard the Rabbi so rattled and told him to sit down. Commander Williams also told him to sit, but to no avail. Sebastian was concerned when the Rabbi continued to shake.

"Rabbi," he said, "take it easy. Would you like a coffee?"

Sebastian was on his third since arriving at the Paradise Motel. He was dependent, and the senior police were the same. They were all close to the coffee machine. Being at a safe distance away from the inner perimeter, as they liked to call it, they had no need to keep their hands full with semi-automatic weapons.

"No thank you," said the Rabbi, taking a soothing bite from his chocolate bar.

"Rabbi, we've met," said Commander Williams, and the Rabbi remembered with some horror the dead body of a young Jewish officer who was new in the job when stabbed at a domestic.

"We have," replied the Rabbi, still searching for his usual aplomb.

Williams soldiered on. "We must follow protocol," he said, gesturing towards a seat. "I've got questions for you, a debrief. This is my 2-i-c, Inspector Ruthven. We're recording you, and he's taking notes."

Sebastian's eye rested on the recording equipment, and his heart crashed against his ribs. *You are charged with possession and administration of drugs.* He reached for his pulse, then for his pills. Sebastian was adept at concealing this move – he had the coffee to wash them down – and Williams had long ago lost his powers of observation. He tried to soothe himself. That was different police, he reminded himself, it was another country, and Williams couldn't track an elephant through snow.

Today Bob Williams had an important role. Sonia was busily multitasking and she had no option but to rely on him. Bob was not to be confined in his authority to traffic and pizzas. He stood tall, and acted with freedom and a return of gut instinct.

"Rabbi, do you understand?"

The Rabbi had been through this previously, but back then there seemed to be efficiency and protocol. He was not at all sure about Bob Williams. He looked at Sebastian for reassurance and then nodded his assent. Williams clicked into action.

"Rabbi, who is he?"

"He said he was Moshe, otherwise I've no idea."

"What does he want?"

"He wants you to shoot him."

Oh no. Sebastian's pulse remained wild and he was back in the hospital. He was young and could run fast with the crash trolley. He got the paddles on the old man's chest and he zapped. The man leapt a foot from the bed and then slumped back down. Sebastian saw the man was himself.

"Well why did he ask for you? Is he Jewish?" continued Williams.

"He looks Jewish, but weird. He knows all about the Torah, he likes to talk. He's circumcised, he showed me."

"What did he want from you?"

"He wants me to do his funeral," said the Rabbi, "and his girlfriend's funeral too. I didn't understand." The Rabbi recalled that Sebastian had made the same request at the Desolation Point Golf Links one week earlier, at the cliff top by the sixteenth tee. He had not known what to say.

Sebastian, feeling uncomfortable, intervened. "Did you agree?"

"I didn't know what to say," said the Rabbi. "Normally I just agree but I don't think he's well. And we have issues with suicide, and tattoos."

Sebastian wondered again why the Rabbi had not agreed to do his funeral when he had asked him at the sixteenth tee. He decided that this was not the right moment to press the point.

"Did you see weapons?" asked Williams, feeling on safer ground.

"No," replied the Rabbi, and felt for his jaw in response to a further stab of toothache.

"Did you see the woman?"

"What woman?"

"Didn't they tell you? There's a woman." Williams was embarrassed because he had acceded to the demand for the Rabbi's visit without extracting anything in return, such as release of a hostage. He hadn't followed protocol and met with the Rabbi before he went in.

"I didn't see a woman," said the Rabbi.

Williams understood that he had made a mistake.

"Well, what else?" he asked.

"Not much really."

"You were in there for half an hour."

"Really?" said the Rabbi.

Sebastian knew the Rabbi was not telling the whole truth. He wondered how and why the strange person had so rattled his friend, who was so capable, even under the weight of the Holocaust.

"Rabbi," said Sebastian, "are there areas that remain confidential – you know, the sanctity of the confessional?"

"No, he just raved on about the prophets, and about death, and told jokes, and cried, and showed me his tatts. I couldn't really engage him, except on the golf. At the Maccabiah Games, Tel Aviv, 1997."

"I remember," said Sebastian. "You went to Israel and we were left here without a fourth for golf."

"How did it end up?" asked Williams.

"He asked for a pizza," said the Rabbi, "a kosher one. I told him I'd pass on his request."

Williams, who knew all about Sebastian's teachings on pizzas in the siege situation, grinned to himself as his 2-i-c wrote "pizza" in his notepad.

"Anything else?"

"He said I'd been no use at all, all he wanted was a Rabbi to do his funeral, and police to kill him."

"Any final words?"

"Yes, Commander. He wants a philosopher to bring him his pizza."

Bob Williams could not immediately think of anything to say about that and all was quiet. His eyes rested on the lunches, while the Rabbi tried to rub his sore tooth. Bob mumbled, "police to kill him", and the Rabbi mumbled, "thou shalt not kill" and "the golf". Sebastian's mind went to the needle and another killing. This time his hand was steady and his patient was grateful and it was good.

6

Back at Desolation Point, Brian and Stefan had played on without Sebastian and the Rabbi, and were now on the seventh, known as *The Duckpond*. But Stefan had been agitated since Sebastian and then the Rabbi were taken.

"Wish the Rabbi was here," said Stefan, and turned his head as he heard for the third time the sounds of an approaching helicopter.

Stefan was not processing information with his usual efficiency, but the police helicopter definitely landed and the man in black emerged, for the third time that windy morning. He examined his watch to try and get his bearings. It was 10.43. How was he going to manage when Brian was taken? He knew Brian to be a forensic dentist who had, during quiet moments in the clubhouse, spoken of his work identifying the unknown deceased. He was going to be left on his own. There'd be three sets of his friends' golf clubs to manage, and no-one to record his score.

Things did not go as expected. "Are you the professor of philosophy at Sydney University?" the man in black asked Stefan in an assertive manner. And then, "Come with me."

Am I really to be faced with death? thought Stefan. And everything went dark for him.

As the police helicopter lifted and flew to the north its passage was observed again by a ragged man and a pelican. This time, both started to rock backwards and forwards in an agitated manner, quite close to the cliff's edge.

* * *

Thirty minutes later Stefan, always prone to blackouts under stress, found himself following Police Dog Schroder up to the front door of the fibro premises. The dog placed something next to the doorway and was called by his handler, leaving Stefan stranded and trying to piece everything together.

So here he was. How did he get here? Where was the Rabbi?

Stefan could see police over where the dog went, poking their guns around the side of the shed. My God, there were guns. Where was Sebastian?

Stefan jumped when the door opened suddenly and he was pulled inside by a heavily tattooed individual who was shirtless. As the man spoke, Stefan's attention shifted from the permanent eyebrows and moustache tatts, to the grand variety of body tatts.

"That Rabbi was useless," the man complained. "All I wanted was for him to do my funeral but he couldn't get past my tatts."

Stefan came to full awareness at the word "funeral". For a moment, he felt that he was in an important role. He was part of a police team, something like a very blokey sports team.

The sitting room was well furnished and tastefully decorated. A Persian rug covered the floor. Stefan shifted in his chair.

"Well what do you think of that, Professor? I know you are a philosopher. I sat in the back row in your Tuesday lectures. Remember, the discussion on suicide bombers."

For a moment, Stefan thought the man to be one of his students. He did recall something about suicide bombers. But all his students wore shirts and he didn't like these tatts.

* * *

Back at the Paradise Motel, Chief Inspector Bob Williams was finishing his early lunch. He would have liked it a bit hotter. Across from Bob, the monitor screen provided a visual feed of the front door of the fibro premises, captured by telescopic lens from the corner of the iron shed. The powerful microphone left by Police Dog Schroder next to the doormat provided an audio feed of conversation discerned through the fibro walls, but Williams was hearing nothing from the philosopher. It was very early days and the other fellow was talking. That was a good thing. He couldn't catch a lot of it but God and death came into it. Probable head noises, he decided.

Bob sat at the trestle table with Sebastian and the Rabbi, who had elected to stay rather than take the return helicopter flight to the golf course. "No, I'll stay," the Rabbi had said, "but could you get one of your officers to retrieve my cell phone from the golf bag, which should be easy for him on his next run. I'm on call for funerals." The Rabbi would feel better once he checked his phone. Meanwhile, he declined the lunch. "I just don't feel hungry," he said.

"I don't know about this, Bob," said Sebastian. "Are you confident about giving in to every demand or request, like sending in the philosopher? Unbriefed?

Just like the Rabbi was unbriefed? You know the philosopher is a civilian with no relevant experience."

Bob looked up and dabbed the gravy from his chin as Sebastian continued. "I'm afraid for him, Bob."

"He'll be right," said Bob.

Sebastian did what he always did these days when his anxiety mounted to panic. He visualised the pelican.

"Hell," said Bob Williams. "I forgot about the pizza."

* * *

Although Bob Williams had finished his lunch, the men in black still crouched behind the corners of corrugated-iron sheds. Sonia was in the police truck, which served as the forward command post. She leant over her audio-visuals. She had a picture on the screen of the front door of the premises, and because of Police Dog Schroder's microphone, there was quality audio. At this moment, however, whatever was being said inside was obscured by the strains of Bach's "St Matthew Passion".

Schroder still wore the camera attached to his collar. He waited for the opportunity to get inside the premises and send back the pictures to Sonia. He watched the men's lunches stacked outside the police truck, foil trays with more foil over the top.

* * *

Inside, Stefan noted the very familiar "St Matthew Passion" and he recognised the weapon behind the door as a .22 calibre rifle, something he had used for shooting rabbits when travelling around the country in his youth. He also saw what looked like a banner but it was part-furled and he could not make out all the lettering. He thought it read *Free Z.* In front of him sat a heavily tattooed man talking death. Usually, Stefan liked a chat about death. This was the way he made his living. But this particular chat had a terrible immediacy about it. Also, Stefan did not like tattoos.

"In your class," the man said, "we studied Socrates. He suicided, didn't he? And we talked suicide bombers in Iraq. But Professor, it was all theory. Let's philosophise a bit with death right here, right now. Suicide is the issue, let's talk suicide."

"Is that gun loaded?" asked Stefan.

Stefan, who thought about death more often than he thought about sex, was nonplussed. He'd woken that morning thinking about suicide and euthanasia, his thoughts centred on his friend in the nursing home. How to assist him? When his fairway wood had gone into the creek on the first hole at Desolation Point, at 7.41 this morning, he had expressed suicidal urges. The Rabbi had been concerned as usual, while Sebastian had laughed at him. Brian the forensic dentist had been uncertain, not having had a lot of exposure to Stefan's suicidal thinking. Then Stefan had said if he had a rope he'd hang himself. But he didn't have one. And besides, there were no trees on the seaside links.

"Yes, it's loaded," said the tattooed man.

Pieces of Stefan's life flashed up. There was his wife, daughters, grandchild, his migrant parents. A childhood of difference, of not fitting in. Despair that he ever would. Yet now he was freed from his daily fears – of ageing, dying, and of helpless incompetence.

The relief did not last. He was shaken by an explosion. His interrogator was thrown across his field of vision. The room filled with smoke. He saw a woman in white, carrying a gun. He definitely saw a dog. He was lifted from the floor and carried to the light. He thought he had heard two shots.

* * *

Noel had not known what to do when he saw the police helicopter fly north for the third time. Pacing the cave had not helped and he did not draw comfort from Donnie's pacing. Then he paced the cliff's edge, where he alarmed some whale watchers.

He went to see Lizzie at the radio room. Donnie followed as far as the radio tower where she had found Noel hanging. She flew off to circle and keep watch from a height.

Lizzie sat with her knitting in front of the radio. Through a glass wall, she had a clear view of Desolation Cove and of the line of cliffs running northward. Her radar screen showed a storm off the coast but heading her way. She surveyed fishing boats that she thought to be too close to the reef. To one side of her desk, a television was silently tuned to Channel 7.

"That pelican tried to follow Sebastian," Lizzie said. "She looked exhausted and I was worried for her."

"Donnie's OK," said Noel. "She's been with me. I'm worried about Sebastian. What has he got mixed up in?"

It was midday and Channel 7 opened with breaking news. The newsfeed informed them there had been light flashes and explosions, and gunshots had been heard at the location of the police siege at Yarramalong. Footage was shown of heavily armed SWAT police storming a farmhouse. One officer had a dog. The screen showed a pudgy man with a stained t-shirt and golf cap entering another building. The camera panned to a sign reading *Paradise Motel*. The camera caught the same individual taking a very large bite from a chocolate bar.

Noel and Lizzie watched in wonder as the news continued. They saw police carry a man in shorts with a large white hat. They scampered towards a waiting helicopter and loaded the man inside. They were quickly followed by two more men in shorts, one pudgy, both with black socks, and both running.

"Sebastian's safe," they said in unison, as the helicopter lifted. Lizzie hugged Noel. He looked unsure of how to respond.

Noel started to pace. "I get so mad at him. He makes me worry."

"Me too," said Lizzie.

"He doesn't know what he's doing," said Noel.

"But he's very experienced."

"Doesn't know when to stop."

"He's done so much good," she said.

"Animals love him – he should have been a vet. He just doesn't get people," said the hermit, and his attention was drawn to Donnie as she flew past the glass wall of the radio room, heading north.

* * *

The police helicopter had reached the coast quickly. Then it was a short cruise south to return to Desolation Point. Sebastian sat with the Rabbi, who had said, "thou shalt not kill" and "golf" several times, but now was silent. They both watched as Stefan, sitting opposite, regained his bearings, and some of his hearing. He had been deafened by the stun grenade.

The noise of the chopper was not too loud inside the cabin and it was possible for those with hearing to talk.

to do? I have no prior experience. But suddenly I've managed it."

The Rabbi spoke to Sebastian. "Do you think he's traumatised? Perhaps you should do something."

"Like what?" asked Sebastian.

"Debrief him," suggested the Rabbi, drawing on his limited knowledge of psychological terminology.

"No, I don't believe in that stuff," said Sebastian. "What he needs is psychological first aid. Getting back to familiar surroundings. Desolation Point."

"Then what?"

"Put a golf club in his hands and see how he goes," suggested Sebastian. "Like me, like the time I got back from a siege and I joined up with you guys on the twelfth."

"I remember you played good golf," said the Rabbi. "But is there some way we can support him psychologically?"

"Of course," said Sebastian. "The tenderness of mates."

Sebastian had been dreading a bad outcome. He'd got through seventeen sieges with no fatalities. Then this. Was it a fatality? He had just been settling in for the long haul – sit it out, negotiate, see what the person wants, talk them down, diagnose if necessary. And now he didn't feel anything really, that's what all the death did to you. After you've had enough deaths, you don't react.

You're half dead yourself. People think it's cruel indifference. But they don't know.

He imagined the fully dead confronting him at night in his dreams, and imagined himself being claimed and taken, to join them. *But hang on, you didn't know this one.* It's the ones you know that confront you. And you don't know if anyone died.

He looked out at the line of sandstone cliffs and promontories running south towards Desolation Point. A pelican had fallen in behind and followed the helicopter. The swell was up, and there was an offshore wind. There was a left-hand break for the surfers on the reef off Desolation Point. The sky was cloudless. "Well, we all got out in one piece," he said.

"Yeah, I'll be glad to put my feet down again on the links," said the Rabbi. "There's still time to play some golf. Golf helps, just like it helped me after that bridge collapse."

"I don't know what to do," said Stefan.

As the helicopter descended, Sebastian could see it was Donnie who was coming in behind. And he could also see the play of wind in the pines by Desolation Cove. A two club wind for the landing. He thought briefly about the Rabbi's report of the superstition about pelicans and death. He didn't believe it. Nevertheless, he made a mental note that he must speak to the Rabbi once again, so that his own funeral could be put in place.

The chopper came low over the lifesavers' radio room and then along by the clubhouse. Sebastian could see Brian by the ninth tee, practising his chipping. Brian waved. The pilot set down gently on the pad by the radio room. It was only a short walk to join Brian but Sebastian paused behind the others, then walked the other way. The secluded spot where Donnie would meet him.

Sebastian didn't use deodorant and once he believed that Donnie's attraction to him was because of his scent. After all she had been up close a lot, back in those days. And she was still keen to get into a touching situation.

Sebastian stopped using shampoo decades ago when a mad hairdresser told him that shampoo made your hair fall out. He'd been fearful that his hair would drop, and then there would be no more wind in his hair. The third world people get on perfectly well with no shampoo. Don't wash away the natural oils, said the mad hairdresser. The natural oils had their distinctive scent too.

Sebastian believed in the pheromones. He did not attribute to Donnie any gratitude, or sense of responsibility, or perseverance, or belongingness. He relied on his scientific training and tried not to attribute human characteristics to Donnie. She's just a bird, they all said. Therefore, he told himself, it was all about the pheromones.

As usual Sebastian did not know what he was going to do next – he liked to think of this state of mind as freedom. Despite his natural reserve, he engaged Donnie with talk of his wife's death and his love affair with the needle.

* * *

I try to be close to Sebastian. I want him to touch me, right on the scars. Sebastian says he deals in damage and a scar is nothing to him. When he visits Noel, I turn up, and I spread my wings in front of the fire.

"You want massage, Donnie?" he asks, and I do.

After the massage I fly higher, I cut back into the winds, I glide and I bank. I feel the wind ripple over the scars and the wings stretch wider. Because I cover the air, I see more too. I don't miss a thing.

Sometimes Sebastian talks to me a lot. He cries and he moans, he gets cross and shouts. I look at him. Eventually he calms down and touches me some more. He still looks sad as he goes back to his golf.

7

"Good to see you," said Brian, as Stefan and the Rabbi approached him on the ninth tee. "I didn't know if I'd have anyone to play with."

Stefan engaged with Brian after a fashion, his hearing gradually returning. Then he collected his golf clubs and started to do his stretches on the ninth tee. His instincts told him to get back to his golf.

The Rabbi needed a moment alone. Once he got himself into the privacy of the locker room, he looked at a mirror. Staring at his reflection he was back at the siege and he became lost in the moment. Coming in behind him was Esther. "You've still got sunblock," she said. "There under your ear. You've had it all through the siege. And you must tell the truth."

"Tell the truth," mumbled the Rabbi, as Esther faded.

Then the mirror filled with the Rabbi's children and grandchildren. And his grandmother, who had rocked and lamented. Then he was with the mob on the terraces at Highbury. Then he headed one home for Arsenal and it was his goal that won the match for them.

He was ready to play golf, and as he walked from the locker room to the tee, he felt his feet as they trod and his muscles as they flexed and the sea wind as it blew upon him.

* * *

Sebastian had settled once he had reconnected with Donnie. He gave thanks that the ninth, known as *Easy Street*, was the easiest hole on the links when the wind blew from the north-east, as it did now. And this was only reasonable, when recovering from a police siege. It was an example of fairness, which normally did not happen on a golf links.

The foursome assembled and stood together on the ninth tee. Except for Brian, none looked happy and each felt fear. They said little but attended serially to hitting the golf ball.

"One hole at a time," said Sebastian.

"Yes," said Brian.

"One shot at a time," said Sebastian, remembering that he advised patients to break things down into manageable portions.

And as they took their further steps into what Sebastian thought of as the golfing kingdom, his mind went back to his first golf at Desolation Point. A small child, he was chased off when the weather was benign, but when the weather blew in from the ocean and scattered the grown-ups, he came into his own. The rain and wind left behind a motley collection of persons who could not be averaged – the serious, the lonely, the totally addicted, the odd golf mystic. Plus there were those who could not pay the fees but came to golf when there was no-one to chase them off.

In those days the golf links was not such a pretty place. Everybody claimed to be hard up, a quid was a quid and not to be thrown away. There was a greenkeeper but no battalions of staff. There was no watering, except on the greens. There was no trimming of edges, tending of flowerbeds or general fussing. A higher value was put on the wild and the uncultured. The long grass went uncut, the windblown bushes remained crooked, and nobody intervened to draw a firm distinction between the sandy knolls, the dunes, and their neighbours, the beach and the ocean.

When the rain did not fall the fairways were brown. When the rains came the lagoon filled, as did the little creeks that were its entrances and exits. The ducks came back, the pelicans too, and one year when Sebastian was in second class with Noel Davies, the black swans nested. These features were all transient, as nature intended, said Noel, just as the tide rose up and left again.

The rain was more important to Sebastian then, for when it rained he could get onto the course. The greenkeeper, a surly man, suspected Sebastian of swiping golf balls from the fairways. He was rumoured to shut small children up in a cage before disposing of them. When his Holden utility was sighted, Sebastian and Noel would run to hide. Sebastian refused to allow his brother Charlie to come and play golf because Charlie, at six years, was a liability, unable to run fast enough to get away from the mean greenkeeper. They didn't have to run far, only to Elephant Rock, or to the second bridge, where the greenkeeper would never follow due to his fear of the brown snake. If the greenkeeper surprised them on the high ground, they ran to the caves.

It was in these caves that Noel and Sebastian had their refuge. In the caves they garnered their strength and put down their foundations.

* * *

Sebastian kept silent for a time as he and Brian played their shots up the right side of the ninth fairway. He needed still to put things behind him, and Brian had the sense not to ask questions about the siege.

"I envy you, Brian. I'd like to deal in teeth. Dental is straight, isn't it – compared to mental? It's too hard for me."

"I don't know, Sebastian. I get some tough ones. The ones who are driven mad by their teeth."

"You would have made a good shrink," said Sebastian. "You're kind and you're practical – unlike my colourful colleagues. You can talk to anyone and you have the rare gift of common sense."

"Thank you."

"But you just wouldn't want to do it, would you? Coping with me is enough."

"I enjoy your company," said Brian.

"I grind my teeth Brian, when I'm asleep."

"Yes," said Brian, "very common. Lots of people grind their teeth. Causes real problems, it does."

"The dentist looked at my teeth – I'd been keeping them away from him – and he said I grind. I was gobsmacked."

"You can get a splint guard," said Brian, "it stops the grinding."

"Yes, my dentist said that, but he said people put the guard in the top drawer, because it's uncomfortable."

"True," said Brian, "there's lots in top drawers now. The grinding does wreck your teeth though. They get very thin at the top and they crack. You get sharp bits and ridges."

"I know," said Sebastian, "it's humiliating."

"Why so humiliating?"

"I thought I was above teeth. You know, somewhere up in the mind. And I'm not Brian. I've neglected the teeth. And I've taken my troubles out on the poor little buggers. The mind didn't do too good, and it decided to grind the teeth. How bad is that?"

"Very common," said Brian.

"But not for a trained psychoanalyst, surely."

"I don't know," said Brian, "I don't know what demons lurk. Some lovely peasants have lovely teeth, not a care in the world, never a worry about their mind, and a lovely mouth. And some educated men in the universities – their teeth are a battle ground – like the Boyne."

"Can you help me Brian?"

"No, I'm afraid you're way over my pay grade. I couldn't possibly help you with that. We humble dentists don't know what drives a man to grind. And we do just palliative care."

"Palliative care?" asked Sebastian, who associated palliative care with dying.

"For the teeth. Palliative care for the teeth."

Brian's benevolence caused Sebastian to think of his working time in Dublin and to give thanks for the Irish alcoholics who had aided his recovery. The Irish Medical Council generously put him in charge of St Patrick's Hospital. "I don't give a toss that you're suspended in Australia," said the chairman, "we need you in St Patrick's. Just stay off the needle."

And he did. When the wind came around from the north-west, it blew the aroma of the Guinness from the factory over the high stone walls and tormented the drinkers. Sebastian understood the drinking man as he understood all addicts, and he was able to give and receive comfort.

Brain and Sebastian reached the green and linked up again with Stefan and the Rabbi, who had both played up the left side of the fairway. The Rabbi appeared to have entered into a different zone.

"They said nothing at all. My grandmother sat there rocking and moaning in Yiddish 'Woe is me, woe is me', and I had no idea why. I thought that's what Eastern European Jews did. They were just refugees. My grandfather was better but he didn't talk about the past. Nobody did. They got on a boat in Poland, they thought they were going to America and ended up in England. That's where I was born. I wish I could ask them questions. I didn't know anything about what she went through until I was a teenager. Then I saw the truth – she was a persecuted refugee."

The Rabbi was gushing, and Sebastian wondered whether he had been able to put the siege behind him. Why is he talking about refugees? He's not telling what he knows about the siege.

The Rabbi flowed on. "I didn't think I'd get back for golf or for today's funeral because of the Qantas strike. Esther was positive as usual. She just said it will work out and it did. We were on the first plane out of Perth yesterday. I was terribly worried, I said to her: 'You don't like travelling with me, do you?' And she said 'no.' You see, I know everything that goes wrong, so I have to leave early for the airport and I have to check the times over and over. I got my courage up and asked her: 'You don't really like being with me a lot of the time, do you, or do you like being with me a lot of the time?' 'Sometimes I like you', she said."

The Rabbi settled over his ten-foot putt and stroked it in for a birdie.

"Rabbi," said Sebastian, "that's Holocaust history, then marital issues, and you're in for a birdie." Sebastian was concerned that the Rabbi had not left behind the Holocaust, but carried it all within him.

"I am a nervous type," said the Rabbi. "My mother was terribly worried about me, and so was my father." He paused. "That crazy man at the siege, Sebastian, I remember now. He told me I couldn't fix the Holocaust. He was inside my mind, Sebastian. No-one can fix it, he said. There'll always be crazy, evil death."

"Sebastian, what did you score?" called Stefan, butting in.

"An eight," said Sebastian.

"An eight," noted Stefan loudly, even though his hearing had returned. He was focused on his golf and strangely free of thoughts of his recent experience. For now.

"Bad luck," said Brian.

"I'm carrying the weight of the Rabbi's counselling session," explained Sebastian quietly, as the Rabbi walked up to the tenth tee and smacked another power fade into the cross-breeze and with a spectacularly good result. "He's onto his nuclear family. I don't know what's gotten into him. He's talking, and it's clearly good for his game."

When they had each hit, Sebastian was able to speak privately to the Rabbi. "What do you suppose your grandfather did?" asked Sebastian. "Did he buy a ticket from a people smuggler and get on a boat in Poland?"

"I don't know," said the Rabbi. "He didn't talk. I guess he fled death and then faced death on the journey. Those who lost family just kept quiet. To be honest I thought the Poles were stupid, like my grandmother. Now I'd like to know her story." The Rabbi walked up to his ball and hit it, no calculation, no practice swing. It came to rest two feet from the flagstick, a guarantee of a further birdie. "I'm on a roll." The Rabbi beamed. "I really should let you put me on the couch."

"They say it's a mental game," said Sebastian.

"I feel relief, Sebastian. I know crazy death will go on, no matter what I do. It's not all up to me." The Rabbi smiled. "I've just got one Holocaust survivor this arvo, I'll honour him. Then the Polish Ambassador's reception tonight. I always get the invite. Grandfather would be proud."

As they reached the green, Brian joined them. "Isn't that Australian flag curious," he said, "sticking up out of the reef like that, as though to welcome boat people."

"Actually," the Rabbi continued, "I'm quite left wing on refugees – because I am one."

I've always felt like a refugee too, thought Sebastian, and his mind went again to Zak, one of his many refugees incarcerated at Callan Park, and to Zak's faithful sister Leah. *They are boat people, like the Rabbi's grandparents. I must ask them more about their flight.*

"It's what the refugee does with the experience," continued the Rabbi. "Look at me. I use it to try and heal wounds. But my uncle – straight into the ranks of Shin Bet. He became what today would be called a terrorist."

"Another eight for me," noted Sebastian, completing his card. *That's two eights on two holes since the siege.* He stared at the card. *My two easy holes, Easy Street, and then the tenth, The Doldrums.*

Maybe I am affected by the siege. I wish I knew what happened. I can't escape my past either. It's an old jumper and I don't want to let it go.

His mind now settled on Zak and Leah. She had kept coming to him at Callan Park with her question. What does it do to a person if life is one big Holy War? The bio she gave about her brother was also her own. A holy war, the flight from a war zone, then some Aussie schooling, but a searching later on. He'd been to the Imams, she said, and father made him go to the Rabbi at the Central Synagogue. There'd been a gradual withdrawal and obsessive online activities. The rest had been on the front pages of the press.

* * *

When the rains come I'm happy. The gullies run and the lagoons fill with water. I know the rains like I know the winds. I know the storms and I know the waves.

Noel's cave is always calm, but he wants to go out in the rain with his golf sticks, just like Sebastian does. I go after him to watch and be sure, and when the lightning starts I swoop him and make him go back.

8

Sebastian did not like scoring eights, even though his public image was that he was cool about poor scores and really more concerned about higher things – he was just here for the exercise, or the conversation. The truth was, he was competitive. And when he competed well and played good golf, the intrusive thinking was kept at bay.

Right now the golf was bad and the thoughts of death and needles were jumbled. He did not know what had happened at the siege, he did not know if someone had been killed, and his mind could not leave it alone.

"Remind me when are you away at that conference?" said Stefan.

"Next week."

"There'll be conflict."

"I don't want conflict," replied Sebastian.

"It'll be a sensation. I'm envious. Whenever I try to attract attention, nobody notices." Stefan sighed and settled over his ball, went into his mental routine of relaxation, practised his swing twice, withdrew, breathed deeply, settled again, and hit. His ball travelled in a graceful arc into the left-hand water hazard. "This relaxation routine's no good," he said, and fiddled with the chinstrap of his large white hat.

"I noticed," said Sebastian.

"I don't know how hard to try when I try to relax," continued Stefan.

"The paper is in Hobart," said Sebastian. "Don't you think it might get lost because it's in Hobart?"

"No. It's an international meeting, and you're reporting on more than a thousand police with psychiatric problems, and they're dangerous."

"What's your paper about?" asked Brian, coming up to the pair.

"Mad police," said Sebastian, deadpan.

"Oh," said Brian.

"Unable to tell if they're in any danger or not, burned out cases, either too much adrenaline or too little, thinking people are against them, pulling out the weapon at the drop of the hat, not safe to work with or be around, totally averse to any conflict, or else dangerously over-reactive."

"What happened to them?" asked Brian.

"Too much policing," said Sebastian. "Too much crazy death. Like Bob Williams at the siege."

"Who's he?"

"You haven't met him. He was the senior officer at the siege. He doesn't want conflict. He wants to provide food so everyone can sit it out for days if necessary, until there's an agreement or a surrender."

"What if it's terrorism?" asked Brian.

"He found it necessary to call Counter Terrorism, because the guy had the complexion of a jihadi."

"That's appalling!"

"He would have got Jones, who's dangerously over-reactive. She believes in going in hard and early."

"Do you do something for these police?"

"I try to put them out before they do more damage."

"No, I meant treatment. Do you treat them?" asked Brian.

"Most of them don't believe in psych treatment," said Sebastian. "it looks bad on their record, and they don't want to revisit the traumas anyway."

"My grandfather was in the Irish police, he survived that."

"Some do. It's hard to pick the ones who survive and the ones who don't."

"It's a tough role for you then?" said Brian.

"Somebody has to decide who to put out and who can stay. And some police with the head noises go OK, once away from the front lines."

"I suppose they go on the police pension?"

"Wish someone would give me a pension," said Sebastian. "Then I could get away from crazy death."

Sebastian's path was blocked by a murder of crows. They stood their ground and challenged him, as the light glinted on their shimmering blackness.

"You're depressed again, Doctor," said the Rabbi. "You should try Prozac."

"It's reality," muttered Sebastian. "Things fall apart after a while. First things are good, then ordinary, and then bad."

"What school of psychiatry is that?" asked the Rabbi, as a pelican swooped low over Sebastian's head, startling him. For a moment he looked happy but then another pelican came in from the ocean and as it passed low overhead it seemed to leave Sebastian in a further pale of gloom.

That can't be Donnie, leaving me distressed. Briefly, Sebastian thought of the Rabbi's reported superstition about pelicans and the connection with death. His mind went to the two gunshots, then back to the prophecy. There may not have been a fatality. He saw Donnie in the distance and came back to normal awareness, on the eleventh at Desolation Point, the hole they call *The Dog's Leg*. The third hole since the siege. The crows had gone and his path was clear. Still little talk of the siege. That's our conversational skill.

As Stefan went through his prolonged warm-up routine, the Rabbi tried to whisper to Sebastian. "Why do you keep working? For me it's easy. I have to keep supporting the grandkids."

"And you support the Holocaust survivors," said Sebastian. "They really are survivors, aren't they? Like you. For me, I don't know if I'm a survivor. I don't know if I'm going to make it through the day."

* * *

Some of them never look at me, so I like to fly low over their heads to make them duck, just so they know I'm here. It's my territory. They just come for a visit, then they're gone again.

Sebastian looks at me. First thing as he arrives, last thing before he leaves and many times in between. When the wind blows hard, he's looking at me all the time, as I cut the air, spiral up and down, do the down-wind sprint or the up-wind hover. He points where he wants his golf ball to go, allowing for the wind's power, and he looks at me. If he's in the lee, I fly to where his ball will go and show him the wind's power. He waves, nods and smiles. Sometimes he points me out to the others and then they shake their heads.

9

The sun tried to break through thickening clouds and a stiffening nor'easter stirred the waters off Desolation Point. The Rabbi and Brian powered up the slope towards the cliff top that hosted the eleventh green. Sebastian laboured along behind and then paused. He applied sunblock to the tops of his ears and to the biopsy scar on his cheek. He still refused the hat because he needed the wind in his hair to survive.

Behind the green, the whale watchers were gathered. Sebastian dragged himself up the last rise and reached the green.

"Should have been here half an hour ago," said a whale watcher.

"A whale doing backstroke," said another. "Just by those fishing boats."

Sebastian looked and saw the fishing boats anchored close to the reef. The boats rocked as the waves passed under them, before rising and crashing on the reef. They were too close to the reef. "I had to do another police siege," he said.

"We saw the helicopter," said the whale watcher. "Four times."

"I could have got here for the whale but the Rabbi's been slow today, due to arthritis and dilapidation." Sebastian raised his voice to draw the Rabbi into their conversation. "Rabbi, we missed the whale. She's been doing backstroke out by the fishing boats while you've been doing your wild slice and zigzagging back and forth."

"Sorry," said the Rabbi.

"Where's your philosopher today?" asked the whale watcher, biting down on his peanut butter sandwich.

"He's over in the bushes, having trouble negotiating *The Dog's Leg*. How long have you been here today?"

"Since dawn," said the other whale watcher.

"What's your secret," asked Brian, "that you can wait like that?"

"When there are no whales, we watch you golf blokes. It's quite entertaining."

"How many whales today?"

"Just the one."

"Have you seen the backstroke before?" asked Brian.

"No," they said.

"I've never heard of the backstroke," said Brian, who always enjoyed a good story. "Are you sure about the backstroke?"

"I'd be worried about your philosopher," said whale watcher. "Said he wanted to jump last time he was here. Right off the cliff. It was the fade, he said. He was always fading and couldn't stand it anymore. He only faded with the long irons, that's what really got to him. I remember every word he said, because he's the only golfer ever said he wanted to jump off here."

Sebastian looked out again and saw a yacht approaching the reef. When he peered and looked down, he saw the waters in the shallows off Point Desolation were calmer, even attractive. He reminded himself that it was a long drop, and that the rocks were ragged at the cliff's base. "He's not really going to jump," he told them, "it's just that when nothing is in control at least you can say you're going to jump. That's in control, isn't it?"

"Only the first bit," said the whale watcher. "After the first bit you just go down with no control at all."

"Of course," said Sebastian. "That's why he won't jump. Come on, Rabbi. Your putt."

"Don't wait for me," called Stefan. "I'm declaring my ball lost."

The Rabbi's putt from close range scurried past its target and his shoulders dropped. "A wipe for me too," he said. "No score at all."

"And Sebastian," called the whale watcher, "I'd be worried about your hermit too."

Sebastian froze in his putting stroke. He'd not had the mental space to worry about the hermit.

"He's been walking backwards and forwards," continued the whale watcher, "and talking to his pelican."

"Where is he now?" asked Sebastian.

"He's disappeared."

* * *

Only Brian and Sebastian registered scores on *The Dog's Leg*. Sebastian tapped in for a birdie, Brian for a par. The scores were duly written on the card. *I'm not scoring well in the head,* thought Sebastian. I was getting OK but now I've got Noel to worry about. I'll check on him later.

Last week, Sebastian had gone looking for Noel in the rain and had found Donnie scrabbling on an outcrop below the eleventh green. *Why is Donnie scrabbling around on that rocky outcrop?* Is she looking over the edge? And where is Noel? He hasn't gone over, has he?

Sebastian climbed down the path. As he did so, he had a view of the roiling surf below, and the reef offshore where the surfers enjoyed the right hand break which appeared only on a low tide with an onshore wind. The surf crashed against boulders at the base of the cliff. Rounding a point, he had a closer view of Donnie who was now joined by Noel. Sebastian breathed a little easier, but Noel was not OK. He was gesturing as he and Donnie together peered down.

Had someone or something gone over? Donnie seemed to point with her bill. Noel was extending his right arm out and down. A flight of pelicans rose on the updraft, oblivious to the pair's concerns.

"Noel? Noel?" Sebastian called as loud as he could and eventually Donnie nudged Noel, who turned in Sebastian's direction. The rain was heavy now and the sound of the wind made conversation impossible until Sebastian could reach Noel's side. Noel turned to look at him with his one good eye. This eye was wide open and the hair was plastered by the downpour.

"I threw it Sebastian," he shouted. Donnie also turned and nodded. And shifted her weight from one foot to the other.

Sebastian stepped to the edge and looked straight down. The surf crashed and the foam flew.

"What?" asked Sebastian. "What have you thrown? Did you mean to?"

"Or I might have dropped it," said Noel. "I might need it again."

"What?"

"My best club. The one iron, Sebastian."

"The one iron," repeated Sebastian.

"You said I didn't need it. You said it wasn't modern. You said nobody used the one iron anymore."

"That's true," said Sebastian. "It's the hardest club to use, but it does hit low under the wind."

"Under the wind," repeated Noel.

"Nobody in their right mind uses the one iron, Noel. There are new clubs which are easier."

"Easier," Noel said. Donnie nodded.

"You were the master of the one iron, Noel."

"I know, but you told me I should get with the times. I did, Sebastian. I chucked it. But now I want it back."

The three of them, two wet men and a pelican, stood at the edge and looked straight down.

"It's low tide Noel, and still you can't see it. It's gone."

* * *

I just wish that Noel would wash. He hasn't had a wash since last time Lizzie told him, and she doesn't have to be close with Noel like I do. His feet smell awful. And his breath smells like fish, old fish. It helps when he gets out in the breeze, when the wind whistles past the cave. But how often is that? Only when the weather's really bad so there's nobody around, or at the crack of dawn or after dark. When he sits by the heater, the smell gets worse.

When I fly off suddenly, I just want air.

10

The whale watchers followed the golfers' progress towards the adjacent twelfth tee. The Rabbi, angered by his golf, approached the twelfth tee before the others. Technically that honour belonged to Sebastian, the low scorer on the last hole. But it was customary to keep up the pace. The Rabbi teed his ball, took his stance and did his usual waggle. His focus excluded completely the sign indicating the hole was called *The Downhill Slide*. It excluded also the hawk diving for a small rodent to his left. He dispatched his ball with its usual slicing shape, but too much, and onto the wrong fairway. "Fore," he called, and a group of golfers on the adjacent fairway turned, crouched and covered their heads.

"And they ask me why I don't play golf," said the whale watcher as he poured coffee from the thermos.

After Stefan hit from the twelfth tee, Sebastian could see that he had hit a good one, and he took his chance. "I think you've progressed," he said. "I expect you to be in B-grade soon."

"I'm not sure I've progressed," said Stefan, who as usual did not take to encouragement.

"You're clearly still alive, whereas last week you told those whale watchers you were suicidal," said Sebastian. "I don't think I could cope with another death, especially yours."

Stefan said nothing, appearing not to register Sebastian's distress.

"You have progressed," enjoined the Rabbi, "and you haven't talked suicide as much. And that's reflected in your general demeanour."

"Yes," said Sebastian. "You're standing tall, with none of that talk about God on this shoulder and the devil on that shoulder, weighing you down it was. Who could stand up straight under the malefactor and with the divine battle fought around their ears? I'd be ducking for cover too."

"I suppose so," muttered Stefan. "Remember I went away last time thinking that a holiday was the cure for addiction. I was bad." As Stefan talked, his voice and his shoulders lifted.

"You were misery itself," said the Rabbi. "I was worried about you. I'd go home to Esther for coffee and talk about how you troubled me, and she said,

'That's really something, you don't normally get troubled about them. Is he a Holocaust survivor or something?' I said, no, he's a golfer. She said I was an idiot and the reason I was allowed to play golf was to stop all that rot and have a game. Otherwise I could just do more funerals and make more money."

"You're lucky, Rabbi," said Brian, "you have a good woman there. Sounds like love, and commitment. Every golfer needs a good woman."

Sebastian gave thanks that he had Magda's love. She seemed to understand his golf and his talk of Donnie. Quickly, his mind went to Donnie and her mating, about the same time he was getting together with Magda. He hadn't seen it all, but he had gone into the dunes behind the third green one day, when the wind was stilled. A succession of male pelicans, waving their bills about. *You've got to be dreaming*, he had thought as he watched. But no, she lapped it up, as they pushed and chased each other, running with their silly little legs. There were colours around their mouths, like the lipstick department in David Jones. He wanted to laugh but he was accustomed to self-control with all his patients, and he stayed quietly crouched behind the tree, stunted as it was by the salt wind.

She was gone for weeks and he was sad, no matter what numbers of putts had gone down, miracle sand saves performed or successful treaties made with the wind. He asked the Rabbi if he had seen Donnie, but the Rabbi always said, "Who's Donnie?" in his kindly voice. Sebastian became irritated and gave up asking. He knew the Rabbi thought his relationship with Donnie unhealthy, and he started to think the Rabbi odd.

Sebastian, always a problem solver, had gone to Noel in the cliff caves under the fourteenth tee. Noel would know where she was. Acting on his advice, one breathless dawn Sebastian paddled the kayak from the point towards the rock islands. The sea was calm enough but as he rounded the eastern side, away from the mainland, there arose an infectious hum, becoming a rumble, and he saw he had arrived at the breeding colony, just a half kilometre from Point Desolation. Donnie was busy on her own little plot and did not notice him as he stilled the paddles. He could see the two little ones, naked and pink, fed by Donnie and her mate with little bits of regurgitated seafood. He didn't disturb her because he knew his place, and as he rounded towards the north side he breathed again and was happy.

The mating did not last. It doesn't for pelicans, although it had for Sebastian. The babies were looked after in a kind of crèche, while the parents started to get back to normal. When they were eight weeks old, they had their feathers on, and they were flying and practising fishing. Sebastian had twice battled the wind and waves to get up close. Then they flew off before the winter and Donnie was back to her lonely tower and her reconnaissance across Desolation Point. She and Sebastian took up again as though nothing had happened.

Noel thought she was aged about ten at that time. She never went missing again and now she'd be about twenty, well on the way for a pelican. The clever hermit had told Sebastian that pelicans lived to twenty-five in the wild, but one had got to thirty-five in captivity. He wasn't sure whether to classify the Desolation Point Golf Links as captivity, but he knew that Stefan and the Rabbi seemed chained to it. Meanwhile, Donnie showed no desire to leave again, and Sebastian continued to observe and make his mental reports to himself, always keeping an eye on her progress.

The Rabbi had just recently prompted the Google search. He knew Sebastian as a technophobe but gently guided him to look up wind. Sebastian had talked so much of the wind that the Rabbi had grown tired, and Esther had made the suggestion over his miserable diet breakfast. "Yeah, I'm getting sick of it too. Why don't you point him at some research? Then he might go off on his own."

For some unfathomable reason – Sebastian had long since stopped making any serious effort at the fathoming – he had not entered "wind" but "pelican".

He was shocked by the speed of the search results, then he was shocked by the contents. Pelicans had a distinguished record in mythology. And places like Louisiana thought so well of pelicans that they put them on flags. Now he knew why it was that he was drawn to Donnie, and why it was that the little willie wagtail who walked and hopped along with him so hopefully every Tuesday just did not quite excite him.

Sebastian caught himself staring at the willie wagtail and heard Brian talking about good women. He'd moved on to Stefan's good woman. "I think she's lifted you," Brian stated.

"I agree Stefan's lifted but I think it was the tenderness of mates that pulled him through," said the Rabbi.

"No it wasn't," exclaimed Stefan. "I hit a good one and decided there was hope."

"He thinks it was that," said Brian to the Rabbi, "but it was the tenderness. Also he's determined."

"I try so hard," said Stefan. "I played with the other mob yesterday. I had a good score and I pranced around telling people what a great time I was having. I behaved like an adolescent, and I was never good as an adolescent."

"You won't have a good score twice," said Sebastian. "So, won't that fix things up?"

"What if I have a good score again?" said Stefan.

"Magical thinking," suggested Sebastian.

"I'm worried it's an addiction," said Stefan. "Two consecutive days of golf and I get delusional."

"At least you see the truth now," said Sebastian, who was closely acquainted with addiction.

"But I keep doing it."

"Are you powerless to resist?" asked Sebastian, entering his professional mode.

"Absolutely."

"That's a start," said Sebastian. "Do you believe in a higher power?"

"That's a tough one. I'll ask the Rabbi."

"No, don't ask the Rabbi, just ask yourself. Do you or don't you believe in higher power?" Sebastian thanked the twelve-step program and especially the higher power for his own recovery.

"Sometimes I do, and sometimes I don't," said Stefan.

"OK, we can work with that," said Sebastian. "Let's say you do believe. We have two steps covered. You've admitted you're powerless over addiction, and you believe in a higher power."

"I guess that sums it up," said Stefan.

Sebastian pictured the next meeting of Narcotics Anonymous. As usual, he would assist the young ones. He would stand. *My name is Sebastian and I am an addict.* He would tell his story, again, and this would help him, again. "Say, 'My name is Stefan and I'm an addict. I'm powerless. My last game of golf was nineteen hours ago.'"

"Yes," said Stefan, "one game is too many and a thousand games is not enough."

"And do you have a genuine intention to give up your addiction?" said Sebastian.

"Not in the least."

"Then you're just an addict indulging."

"Yes I am, and it's time to hit. Do you mind if I go first?"

"Yes, I do. My ball is further from the green. The etiquette is it's my honour. You have to wait. Just because you're an addict doesn't mean you go first."

"Well hurry up then."

"Hang on, the group ahead is still within range," said Brian.

"Go on, Sebastian," said Stefan. "It's a thousand to one that you'll hit one of them, and we're all insured. If I have to wait, my swing deteriorates."

"You've got withdrawals, haven't you?" said Sebastian.

"I've got everything," said Stefan, mournful again. "Unstable mood, highs, lows, impulsive behaviour, bad dreams. I've turned off the phone so the university can't disturb me. I'm a rollercoaster, hell on wheels."

"Just pretend," suggested Sebastian.

"You've had your moments," said Stefan. "What about that gynaecology exam when you needed three whiskys to get through the front door of the hospital?"

"A special case," said Sebastian. "There were diseased organs."

"And you're not addicted, are you?"

"I am an addict, and I'd relapse if I had to do that again. But I got through."

For a moment, Sebastian was back in his wrecked car, his wife dead beside him. His body was broken but soon there was something for the pain. The downhill slide was smooth. He saw again the needle.

"I hear you're making a charge at B-grade," said the Rabbi, hoping to cheer up Stefan. "You wouldn't believe it, I'm threatening A-grade. You don't have to be that good, you just have to work at it. You can be a self-starter, and it didn't matter that my father didn't play golf."

"Yeah, well my father would have looked a complete alien on a golf course."

"That's alright, Stefan. I didn't want to be seen with my father on a golf course. He would have looked a real sight. Warsaw ghetto meets St Andrews."

"What did he do?" asked Stefan.

"Got to England as a refugee, never played any sport, didn't know what golf was until I told him. I'd like to tell him when I've made A-grade."

"What's this?" said Sebastian. "I've missed this A-grade stuff. What?"

"Me, A-grade," said the Rabbi.

"Remarkable, there must be a God after all," said Sebastian. "What's this about fathers?"

"Our fathers were aliens until we got to know them," said Stefan.

"No, that's not quite right," said the Rabbi. "Mine was earthy enough, he just would have been an alien on the golf course. But normal. Part of a community, doing his best to raise a family."

"Was he a Rabbi too?" asked Sebastian.

"No way. Rag trade in North London. We don't do that hereditary rabbi stuff."

"You seem so orthodox."

"No, I'm officially unorthodox. What about your father?" he asked Brian.

"My father taught me to play as a kid, back in Cork. It was important for my social advancement, to get away from the Gaelic football and the hurling."

"And what about your father, Sebastian?" asked the Rabbi.

"Fifth generation Australian," said Sebastian. "Still seemed alien. But he owned a set of golf clubs."

"Did you play with him?"

"Yes, right here in the desolation."

"My father couldn't have done that," said Stefan.

"No-one took me out," said the Rabbi, "until a uni mate showed me."

"Weren't you shut up in Rabbi school or something?" asked Sebastian.

"No, it wasn't like that. I was at uni in London and then rabbi school later."

"They ever let you out?" asked Sebastian.

"Of course. I think you have the wrong idea."

"I have this image of black hats and ringlets in front of the ears, and much rocking backwards and forwards, and much disputation about the Midrash and the Talmud and all that stuff, and hereditary positions for rabbis."

"Dad didn't even want me to do it," said the Rabbi. "He said it was hard to make a buck as a rabbi, and they'd want to own me. Granny was pleased though. Rabbi was big time in Poland. She even stopped lamenting for a few minutes when I told her I was going to rabbi school. You've got it all wrong, those guys with the ringlets are crazy. If I was one of them I wouldn't be allowed to play golf."

The group of golfers in front moved out of range. Sebastian hit a good one and Stefan hit a C-grade shot into a bunker. "It's alright for you," he said, "you had golf clubs at home and a father who knew what golf was."

"They were Depression era golf clubs," said Sebastian. "There were five in a set, all hickory shafts, and Dad thought the five were a luxury. He said you could play a round with just one, the five iron. So we'd set off, dividing up five clubs between us, which was never going to work out equitably.

Noel and I got two each so Dad could set an example about what it was like in the Great Depression and how you could get by with less. And I still feel like that – can't shake it off. I've got fourteen clubs but they're not flash and I feel I have to use every one of them every time to justify owning them."

"I had noticed but I wasn't going to say anything," said the Rabbi. "You should invest in your game. These new clubs are lifting me into A-grade."

The golfing foursome continued walking on the *The Downhill Slide*. Donnie remained on her tower. Nearly four holes had been played since the siege. The Rabbi was resilient. Stefan looked normal.

Sebastian chased off his thoughts about dead bodies and needles.

One hole at a time.

He concentrated upon *The Downhill Slide*.

* * *

They start standing tall, chatting away. Then they slump and they trudge. When they come back to where they started they look defeated. They go away but back they come.

Noel's a bit of an old grot. His toe nails are bad and he hardly ever shaves. His feet smell. He shies away from people and they shy away from him too. There are no friends.

I know what it's like getting old. Your feathers start falling about and your joints go crackly. It hurts a lot and you miss your step. The wings don't work properly. A low wind landing on a light tower becomes a bingle with a metal pole. They all look at you – and not in a nice way.

I really like Noel. He saved me. He gave me refuge, he gave me pears and fish. I don't mind now that he mutters. I protect Noel. He walks close to the edge.

I really really like Noel, but the other old people drive me crazy.

11

Sebastian wanted to be an A-grade golfer just as the Rabbi did. The truth was he had difficulties with the transition from police psychiatrist to B-grade golfer. In the former role, he was cautious and professional, caring deeply about possible error. The same applied to his role as psychiatric assessor of returned jihadis at Callan Park Mental Hospital. In the golfing role, he was bold. He didn't care about getting it wrong. He liked to try the difficult shot, rather than the conservative shot. But his choices were often wrong. That was why he was a B-grade golfer, yet an A-grade psychiatrist on his CV. He continued to work at finessing the transition.

The clouds were thickening as the foursome came down the twelfth fairway.

"How do you adjust to golf after a siege?" asked Stefan. "It just seems so unreal now. I've never been in a siege before. It's left me jittery. I can't play golf if I'm jittery. I've blown the eleventh and now I'm in trouble on the twelfth. I'll never make B-grade. I know what's going on my tombstone. *He never made B-grade.*"

Sebastian didn't think he was up to engaging Stefan on the siege, so he said nothing.

"I've blown nearly every hole," said Brian, trying to be helpful, "and I haven't even been in a siege."

"You're certainly in a predicament there." The Rabbi pointed to Stefan's ball where it had come to rest in a deep bunker. He was looking particularly plump and happy, now that he had put the siege behind him.

"What about you, Rabbi? How do you cope after a siege?" asked Stefan.

"You concentrate on the ball," said the Rabbi. "Look at the dot at the back of the ball, and dismiss thoughts about sieges. And when you are standing in the sandpit, keep the knees bent, and keep them bent as you hit through the ball."

Some time back the question was, "Why would you want to play golf after a siege?" or "Why would you want to play golf after a terrorist assessment?" or "Why would you want to play golf at all, when you could be engaged in other productive pursuits?" That question seemed completely churlish to Sebastian, put only by people who hated golf for one reason or another. Now the question was, "How best to enjoy the golf?" When assessing a terrorist, assess the terrorist – when at the golf, be at the golf.

Stefan took a swing, kept his knees bent, made good contact, and watched happily as the ball scooted down the twelfth fairway.

"Well hit," said the Rabbi, then added, "I did find it hard at first. The police chaplaincy, the deaths there, it all got mixed up on the golf course. But Esther said I was neurotic about it and I should just concentrate on the golf when I was at the golf. So I do. She said that I had to keep myself in shape, despite all the death, to do more funerals. We need the income apparently. It's all the grandchildren."

"I don't have grandchildren, but I still need the golf," called Sebastian. He surveyed his next shot as he approached his ball on this lengthy par five twelfth. A hundred and fifty metres to a flag that was tucked behind a bunker. The conservative approach was to the left, where the green was open. Sebastian resolved to hit a high fade to the right, over the bunker, and stop it abruptly before it ran off the back of the green. "I've always needed the golf," he said. "I need you guys too. I need to tell you things, it stops me worrying, and I need to see how bad you are at golf."

He didn't say that he also needed Donnie, who inhabited a world beyond police sieges and terrorists. He also needed the clever hermit. Sometimes he told the hermit about his problems, for Noel too seemed in a space beyond sieges and terrorists. Noel plus Donnie equals sanity. But he didn't say this out loud, for he was uncertain whether the Rabbi would get it.

Without a practice swing he took the high stakes option. His ball flew, and he soared with it. Alas, it came down a metre short and embedded itself in the face of the bunker, an impossible position. It had flown close to glory but did not quite arrive.

"Bad luck," said Brian, "but a good try. You're such a gambler. Why don't you ever try the safe option?"

"It's what I do at work," said Sebastian.

Stefan took the lofted iron but struck the ball as he took a practice swing. It travelled six feet sideways.

"If I had a gun I'd shoot myself," he said. "Has anybody got a gun?"

"Not me," said Brian, making a show of feeling all his pockets.

The Rabbi muttered under his breath.

"I couldn't cope," said Sebastian. "I shot a kangaroo once and I've regretted it ever since."

Stefan picked up his ball, giving up completely.

"What would your mother say if she heard you talking about shooting yourself?" said Sebastian.

"She's dead."

"Yes but what if she were here?"

"She'd be demented, wouldn't recognise me."

Talk of demented mothers upset Sebastian and his thoughts turned and tumbled towards his own mother. It was the needle again, and it relieved her distressed breathing. She came to be at peace. Then he was lost in her ashes. How surprising that a woman who feared the wind should end up here at Desolation Point, her ashes going this way and that, now with the hang-gliders in the updraft from the cliffs, then circling in a spiral with the pelicans, then still for a moment and settling on his golf ball as it curved like a skater before hitting a wall of wind and dropping like a stone. Sometimes he could see her, when the light came at a certain angle and reflected off the sandstone. But the Rabbi couldn't see her. "Your mother's long dead," the Rabbi always said. "Obviously you won't see her now."

Sebastian was looking skywards. The wind had shifted and the clouds were thickening again.

"Are you OK?" asked Stefan, and Sebastian gathered himself.

"But what if," said Sebastian, rising to the challenge. "What if your mother did recognise you as her son."

"She'd say, 'Go for it. Here, I'll pull the trigger. It'll save you from a horrible end like I'm having.'"

"Rabbi," called Sebastian, "talk to this person."

The Rabbi, who was to do a funeral later in the afternoon, wasn't in the mood. "Don't talk death at me. Why does everybody pick on me? Death, death, death. Yada, yada, yada. Why don't you go and do something useful? Have children, populate the land."

"I've done my duty, and then Jenny wouldn't let me in the bed until I had the snip," said Stefan.

"A curse on the both of you," said the Rabbi. "Your duty is to populate."

"Why?" said Stefan. "Then there'd be more of us having a bad time."

"No, no. Children don't have a bad time," said the Rabbi. "They bring joy as we watch them travel their own paths. No more of this tomfoolery." He gave his golf ball an angry smack with his lob wedge, right on the spot on the ball where it said Mercedes Benz – he'd been given the ball at a charity day. The smacked ball flew high and landed close to the flag.

"Tomfoolery," said Sebastian. "That's what my mother said when I talked nonsense. My dad called it 'phooey and plut', and I never heard anyone else say that. You're talking phooey Stefan, and plut. I'm not into tea and sympathy. No-one ever promised me a good time. You're here to hit the golf ball, whether it goes in the hole or not. Picking your ball up just now incurs a two stroke penalty. You can't pick up the golf ball without marking the spot."

Stefan looked aghast and Brian frowned.

"There are no exceptions for suicidal golfers," said Sebastian. "Nothing in the rules about that at all. The rule book is quite clear." Sebastian felt a speech coming on and found the power of it lifting him up and taking him before he could think. "If you're a bit suicidal over a one shot miss, then a two stroke penalty should clinch it. And if there is still doubt then just keep playing golf. You'll hit the depths."

A lone black crow wheeled out of the ominous skyscape and passing close to Stefan's golf bag, gave out a long and loud "Quark". Stefan startled. "What was that?" he asked.

"I think that was God saving me from a very bad speech," said Sebastian.

"That wasn't God," said the Rabbi.

"Maybe just a messenger," said Sebastian, again lifted up before he could think.

The Rabbi looked at him thoughtfully.

Sebastian's attention was diverted by a resonating peel of thunder. "Saved," he said.

The twelfth was completed with some urgency as the foursome became aware of threatening clouds on the horizon. Brian and the Rabbi were happy to record bogies.

Sebastian managed an unlikely save from his difficult position in the bunker, and walked off with another par. He was back. The scores were recorded and at this stage, he gave himself an even chance of getting through the day.

Stefan had left the group on the green and gone off to the thirteenth tee. By the time the others joined him, he had organised some of his wet weather gear and the rain had started to fall. "Thank God it's raining," he said, taking the plastic trousers from his golf bag.

Sebastian felt a freshening of wind and took his mother's woolly jumper from his bag. As he aged he'd found himself easy prey to memories, especially in the wind and rain. A few drops of rain now, and his memory was away. He always loved the wind and did not understand his mother's fear. Secretly he thought it a bit on the pathetic side. "But why do you like the wind?" she would ask, as he nursed her. He didn't know how to say that it kept him alive and would try to say something concrete, like "It improves my golf". "Do you play golf?" she would ask, and then she would remember Noel.

When the wind howled, she stayed indoors. Looking back he could see it was fear. He hadn't known then, but Noel was on to her. She came out to watch Noel and Sebastian play in the under 14 championships. Noel was the champ. Sebastian had started going the way of education but Noel wouldn't have any of that. The north-east wind started up in the afternoon when they were on the last few holes and Noel was about to win. Mum went home when the wind got up. Dad stayed. Sebastian just put this out of his mind, an unconscious sort of kid. Noel said later he'd be no good at psychiatry because he didn't know anything about his mother.

They were different days then. Nobody had official phobias, or anxieties, or doubts about their identity. Or they never said. Sebastian was a swot, Noel was a jock, Mum was a mum. The whole thing was clear.

The wind blew, Mum went in and Noel went out – to the most exposed part of Desolation Point, just above where he lived now. He'd practise his wind shots. Sebastian would go sometimes, and other times he stayed with his Mum and did his homework – now he was a scholarship boy. He didn't love the wind like Noel did, at least not then. Noel saw it better because even then he so loved the wind. Sebastian learned to love it later, when life was harder and the wind was a friend, just as Noel always said it was.

Sebastian had said his goodbyes to Noel slowly. He put his head down to study as Noel put his head down to golf. Their shared determination took them apart. Sebastian went to medical school and Noel went on the road, an Australian champion set to take the world. By the time Sebastian graduated, Noel had been blown off his cliff at Hoylake, and had then fallen gracelessly. As Sebastian became busier and busier, Noel failed in rehab, relapsed, and stalled. There was a re-connection when Noel attempted suicide but Sebastian was more the doctor than the friend. The downhill slide continued until Donnie appeared by some miracle and Sebastian came to love the wind as Noel did.

As the weather blew in the socialites went off the course, leaving the truly motivated, the obsessed, the mad, and the intoxicated. Sebastian saw in his mind's eye the links of sixty winters. He remembered his father's way – "You must hit under the wind" – and he remembered Noel Davies, club champion before the breakdown, who believed the wind was his friend. "You have to hit it right out over the water and trust in the wind to do the work with you and bring it back. Don't fight with the wind." And he knew the modern way, to cut or draw the ball into the crosswind, so that the wind was nullified and there was a nil result, the final reckoning was as though the day were calm.

The wind was the same wind – untended, uncultivated, unknowable – and the characters it blew in were the same as ever, the hovering hawks, the flapping pelicans, and the lone golfers, head down to cut the resistance, purposeful.

"Oh yeah," Stefan would say, with a doubtful and suspicious air. Stefan did not believe that Sebastian cut the ball into a crosswind to produce a straight result but persisted in his belief that a ball well struck will fly straight. "You don't believe the evidence of your own eyes," Sebastian would tell him. "If you don't believe me, perhaps you'll hear it from Noel one day."

What a shock when his mum died. She wrote her own eulogy – wouldn't trust anyone else to get it right – and Sebastian had to read it out. *I have always had one great fear in life, the wind, and for that reason I want my ashes scattered to the wind, so that in death I can conquer that fear and be as free as the wind. And when my loved ones feel a little breeze they will know it is me watching.*

"I love the rain," said Stefan as he pulled on his favourite plastic trousers.

"It's certainly raining, and it's darkening," said Sebastian. "Let's get a move on while we can. We'll have to get off the links if there's lightning."

"The rain cuts out the day trippers and the holiday types," said Stefan. "The sun comes out and out they come again, cluttering up the golf course, thinking it's just some kind of a game."

Sebastian looked about and saw that most golfers were heading for the clubhouse. He saw Noel Davies coming out from his cave below the fourteenth tee and he was reassured. Noel was seen on the links only when the weather blew in from the sea. "There's Noel, and he's heading for the fifth fairway," he said quietly. But he wasn't sure if his eyes deceived him. He looked again and saw that a lone pelican trailed him. Then he knew it was Noel. He reminded himself that Noel was always drawn back to the fifth and sixth. These were for Noel the hardest holes at Desolation Point, known to the members as *Tragedy* and *Ambush*.

"I've never seen him before," said Stefan. "I didn't believe he was real."

"He's real," said Sebastian, as Noel hit a long iron through the gloom and onto the fifth green. "Noel is the golfer's golfer," he said. "You go to Noel if you lose your way and need help."

"I should go to him," said Stefan.

"No, you'll startle him and he'll be back to the caves."

"Could you introduce me, organise an appointment, or something? I read all the books, all the golf magazines, I take lessons, I talk to the Rabbi, and still I'm stuffed. I'm willing to do anything, except give it up."

"Hit the ball," barked Sebastian.

As Stefan hit his ball he didn't notice a baby rabbit scurry for cover behind him, nor that three pelicans came together to settle on the lamp post outside the clubhouse. Sebastian noticed. He had never before seen more than two pelicans on that post. A special day, he thought, and he tried once again for the special golf shot.

Sebastian's cut shot into the crosswind finished on the short grass.

"You're in the mayor's office," said Brian.

Stefan's straight ball, well struck, had been carried on the wind and into the long grass.

Sebastian turned to Stefan. "I'll introduce you one day. You can ask Noel about existential dilemmas, like whether to give up golf."

Stefan thought this a reasonable suggestion. After all, a rabbi and a psychiatrist had not been able to help. Perhaps this hermit had something. Stefan was a searcher. That's why he became a philosopher and not an engineer like his father. Still he wondered whether he was good enough, as a philosopher or as a golfer. But he was always prepared to take advice.

Stefan had to walk away from the group to reach his wayward ball, and Sebastian was concerned that he might start thinking about the siege. In fact, Stefan thought first about golf – such a difficult relationship. Is it love? He was not an athlete, and grew up feeling out of the mainstream. He had found no comfort in male sports teams, except in this extraordinary foursome, where he could be suicidal and accepted. He could be tactless, yet well liked. And he didn't have to teach anybody about death and euthanasia.

But as Stefan approached his wayward ball in the long grass, his mind drifted to his own ageing, dying, death, helplessness, and incompetency. These were his daily concerns. He was glad to be with the Rabbi for his kind perspective, and with his old friend Sebastian who understood him without using psychiatry on him.

There was a brief flash of the siege, and Stefan thought he could see the perpetrator sitting in the back row of his lecture room, but he let it go. He was assisted by the increasing rain. In heavy rain, he needed all his powers of concentration to play decent golf. A good downpour restrained the head noises. And he thought he was better for the siege, better for a dose of genuine senseless violence, maybe even death.

Sebastian and the Rabbi watched from the other side of the fairway and were reassured when Stefan swung his club. While Stefan watched the flight of his ball, his body language remained positive.

Sebastian was alone as he walked up Pensioners Hill in the rain, and he searched again for his bearings. What am I afraid of? Crazy death and Noel topping himself. And Stefan too – I'm still afraid.

Everybody has fears. Noel feared coming second or not winning, even though he has forgotten that now. Mum feared wind. Stefan feared death and illness. His solution was to philosophise about it – death, suicide and euthanasia. The Rabbi feared persecution and the Holocaust. His solution? He gave eulogies for Holocaust survivors when they died, and collected the eulogies together so that there was an answer.

Noel doesn't seem to have a fear now. It's all mystic fascination with birds, his friendship with Donnie, the sculptures, his support of creatives. He says, it's all about the beauty. He doesn't remember that once it was all about winning. Even when the weather's really bad and he's out there playing the tough holes, it's the beauty of the long iron curving in the wind, the hawks hovering as he hits, and Donnie trailing behind with her own special beauty. He's dropped the fear.

It's the survival that keeps me going, Sebastian thought. No pension for me, I'm not so lucky as those police who go on the pension. My salvation is that these golf guys continue too. And Donnie, who's stronger for the trauma. And Noel, who's transformed by his.

Zak was transformed too – in a bad way. He'd gone a great distance beyond teenage rebellion and he was stuck in a world view of victimhood and of jihadis versus the rest. He did not have the resilience to put aside real or imagined sleights against him. There was no evidence that he was disillusioned by his experience of Islamic State. His shining cause ruled him, and he was unprepared to examine the war within himself. Sebastian told Zak that they both prayed to the same God, and Zak had glared at him.

Sebastian did not know how to change the young man's world view, merely how to keep him from a dangerous environment and to restrain his capacity to act violently.

* * *

When there's a storm now, I get frightened. It's the flash of light first and then the noise. I always make the trek to Noel, quick smart. Sometimes I see Sebastian playing in the rain and I fear for him too.

While the storm rages, I put my head on Noel's lap, and he talks about the beauty. He knows all the details about the reef, and the cliff, the cove and the links. He knows Desolation Point as well as any man can, without flying.

It's when everything's still that his demons are raging and he's walking up and down muttering. I wish he wouldn't walk so close to the edge of the cliff. He's old now, and his balance has got worse, like my flying. When he walks up and down, I walk with him and it's hard to keep up because his legs are longer. I lean into him when I do catch up and I remind him I'm there. I walk on the ocean side so he won't fall.

12

The rain became heavier as the foursome trudged the thirteenth fairway up Pensioners Hill, after which the hole was named. Brian and Sebastian had hit their seconds to the right, Stefan to the left. The Rabbi, a left-hander, sliced one and so joined Stefan on the left.

"You're playing really well, Sebastian."

Brian saw the good in one, the bright future or the chink of light, when others saw only the shadow and the thirty days of continuous rainfall. He saw too that Sebastian was again troubled by a shadow.

"Brian, do you know where the pelicans go in really bad weather?"

"No, I do not."

Sebastian stoically continued his push through the squall at ten per cent incline with his pulse rate quite alarming at 150. There was no sign of Donnie. At least there was no lightning.

"Do you have pelicans in Dublin?" he shouted above the wind.

Brian shook his head sadly.

"Do you like pelicans?"

"I've never thought too much about the pelicans."

"I was like that once," said Sebastian, "but now I'm that mariner who needs an albatross to keep himself sailing through the waves. I need Donnie."

"Mm," said Brian thoughtfully. "Today you've recovered and you're winning, unaided right now by any pelican."

"So you say, but we haven't finished. It's hard going with water in the shoes and I'd be really happy with an honourable draw."

"But you're back from the dead Sebastian, and now you can win," declared Brian, a man who revelled in good news. He had the capacity to enjoy life, even while identifying dead bodies at the Glebe morgue.

"Brian, this is a rule of golf. I don't win." Sebastian felt himself sinking under the poison weight of his own conversation and tried a new tack. "Did you play the hurling?" He'd been wanting to ask somebody that question for years.

"No," said Brian, "the teachers made me do the Irish dancing."

Sebastian lifted momentarily. He reached his ball and gave it a good hit. As it landed with a splash upon the thirteenth green, another squall blew in directly from the ocean, striking the cliff face where he imagined Donnie to be huddled. The squall then swept across the top of Desolation Point and took with it the remaining flotsam and jetsam of the midweek golfers. All now went to retire indoors, save the melancholic and the mad.

Brian and Sebastian were joined by the Rabbi and Stefan, who had come in from the left. The foursome stood solid together against the elements. "Good hit," shouted Brian across the squall.

There he goes again, thought Sebastian. Doesn't he know that defeat is coming? Then quickly he thought, what a lovely man, he still talks to me in spite of everything.

"Sebastian, the front page of your scorecard is wet. The water's been running from my jacket into my pocket and look, the ink's run. See the cobalt smudge just here, looks like a mouse."

Brian's ball reached the thirteenth hole, which was filled to the brim with rainfall. His ball floated rather than dropped, and when the wind picked up, it blew off and kept going, all the way off the green and down the fairway slope.

"I'm scoring you as in the hole," said Sebastian, who again assumed the rules to be for ordinary people.

"I'm writing it later when we're back inside and dry. Just remember your score, or make it up later."

At this point, the world turned once again. A siren sounded, the first sheets of lightning struck Point Perpendicular to the north, and the police helicopter appeared from below, rising over the cliff top before landing on the thirteenth green.

"Oh, for God's sake. What now?" exclaimed Stefan, his charge towards B-grade again interrupted by police.

"The greenkeeper won't be at all happy," said the Rabbi. "That's four greens damaged in one morning."

"I believe it's my turn," said Brian, moving to board the police helicopter. He noted the time at 1.55.

Sebastian's heart sank, for he knew that if Brian was needed, it was to identify a deceased person.

"That's the siren to get off and take cover," said Sebastian. "Nobody plays in the lightning."

Stefan and the Rabbi were in full retreat. Sebastian was uncertain whether he was heard when he called out that he was taking refuge in the cave under the cliffs. There he could connect with Noel. He knew that Noel would retreat from the lightning. "See you guys back on the fourteenth tee when the all-clear siren goes off."

Before the first sheets of lightning lit up the cliff, Sebastian was zipping up his golf bag. He did not see the pelican glide down and below the edge as she headed for her home.

* * *

Sebastian clambered down the rocky path and approached Noel's cave from the ocean side rather than from the lee. He was surprised to see Donnie there and she looked surprised to see him too. She stood tall with her wings outstretched, warming herself by a driftwood fire. The underside of her right wing still showed the scarring from the lightning strike.

"Donnie, I'm OK."

Donnie nodded her great bill and gently flapped her wings.

"She comes to me when there's lightning, or about to be lightning," said Noel, as he emerged from the rear of the cave.

"I'd been wondering," said Sebastian.

"Sometimes the lightning never happens. We just look at each other like we did when I nursed her, and then she's off again when she realises her mistake. I'd be cautious too, and I've come back where it's safe, haven't I?"

Sebastian noticed Donnie was standing next to a mobile phone and he looked at Noel questioningly.

"I know what a mobile phone is," said Noel. "Lizzie left it. She said it's good to be connected." He pushed at the pile of driftwood burning at the mouth of his cave. "I don't need connection, I have what I need."

Noel looked about. There was a couch and one rock wall was covered in framed photographs of his win at the Australian Open in 1967, right here at Desolation Point. He was putting the final green, the wind up that day and ruffling his shirt and trousers. A fresh-faced amateur, he had been just seventeen. Sebastian was in the background carrying Noel's golf bag. His hair was windblown. Sebastian's mum and dad were there cheering. A pelican hovered. In the background rose Point Desolation.

"No-one needs to contact me Sebastian, although it's nice to see you."

Sebastian moved in close between Noel and Donnie and warmed his hands over the fire. He looked out to sea for the whale migration, as was his habit when he started to feel the cold.

"The whales haven't started yet," said Noel, reading Sebastian's mind. "You're feeling the cold because there's a low pressure system, but it's only mid-May, the water's still warm. Next week maybe you'll see the whales."

Sebastian considered this a true explanation. He knew those whale-watching blokes were having a lend of him.

"I don't want to be contacted," continued Noel. "People live in cages but here I'm free, like the birds."

He gestured out the mouth of his cave where obligingly, a pair of hawks hovered.

Sebastian had lived with the fear of Noel topping himself. He checked each week and when he was anxious in between, he rang Lizzie at the surf club. She had news of Noel doing a shift in the radio room – he just had to look out for any trouble and raise the alarm. Sometimes she checked him out in his cave because she also had anxiety about finding Noel's dead body.

Occasionally he rang Hugh the barman for an update, because Noel always came by at closing time for the leftovers. He brought back the empties with him, basically because he was neat and looked after his cave. Hugh would tell Sebastian, "Yes, he came last night as usual." Really it was a better system than having the Red Cross or the district nursing service.

Sebastian had attended several patients in caves over the years, even before the closure of the mental hospitals. They always told him that everybody other than themselves lived in cages.

"Don't top yourself, Noel," he had said, and Noel had replied, "Don't you top yourself, you're the one with all the pressure." Sebastian reminded Noel that he was the one who had actually done it.

"I don't remember a thing," said Noel.

"You left a note."

"It won't happen again. Now I'm free." As Noel gestured out the mouth of his cave, Donnie followed his eyes, momentarily watched the hawks, then settled back to Sebastian.

"Noel, it was a man wanting to suicide, just like you did, except he wanted the police to shoot him."

"He's a bastard for behaving like that," said Noel. The tone of his voice made Donnie look at him. "You know, he's drawing others into his problems. Look, he's even upset you."

"He didn't seem rational, just like you weren't rational when you did it."

Donnie started to move her head rapidly back and forward as she looked from Noel to Sebastian and back again, and to rock from foot to foot.

"I don't know what state I was in. I don't remember anything before you were looking after me in the hospital. But this bloke, wanting police to shoot him and getting you out there, when I know you can't take another death. Even if I was suicidal, I wouldn't – for you."

Sebastian breathed a sigh of relief and Donnie relaxed so that her wings dropped to her sides. "I value my second chance. I care for what I've got."

"I think there may not be a second chance for this bloke," said Sebastian. "I heard two shots, and now they've taken the dentist."

Noel nodded. "I have to care for you too. I'm not sure that you're a survivor like me."

"Thank you," said Sebastian. When he looked again, Noel had fallen asleep on the couch. He was still a bit wet and his breathing was laboured. Sebastian let him be, but covered him with the rug that Sebastian's mother had crocheted just for Noel. Then he spoke out loud about further details of the siege and of what the Rabbi had said about pelicans. Donnie listened again as the doctor unburdened. Together they watched over the clever hermit as the rain fell like a curtain and the lightning lit the ocean horizon.

"I try to believe in miracles, Donnie," he said.

Miracles had come upon him from an early age. He always could run from the greenkeeper and the black swans nested at Desolation Point when he was in 2nd class. Then Noel won the Australian Open as a seventeen year old and Sebastian, accepted into medical school, participated in the miracles of birth and of life. Back at Point Desolation, whenever he could get there, the wheel of nature turned. He always felt watched and protected, he said. He just had to jump in the deep end and somehow he could swim.

He removed his shirt to dry it by the fire. Donnie gaped at his scars. There was the surgical incision straight down his back and the thicker curved scars at both hips and disappearing beneath his shorts. Down his chest a long scar had turned keloid but its roughness did not compare with the crests and hollows of the childhood burning which traversed his neck and shoulders. Her eyes rested on the burning and then she lifted her wings to reveal her scars.

Again Sebastian was encouraged. "I try to believe in the miracle of life," he said.

* * *

The police helicopter landed on a wet university oval and Brian transferred from it to a black vehicle. The siren pierced his ears during the short trip down Parramatta Road to the morgue.

Still in his wet clothes, Brian assumed his normal routine. All cases deserved equal time and respect. He stirred two teaspoons of Maxwell House coffee, two sugars and two whiteners in the fairly clean mug. He exchanged happy words about the rugby with the troops. It was important to keep up morale.

"Hey, Brian," called Gloria the fingerprint girl. "They want you to get on with it – something about national security."

"Oh do they?" said Brian. "What about that terrorist's bomb when six families claimed ownership of the same mangled body? I had to take my time to get that one right."

He put aside his mug and examined the police report. An unidentified terrorist, it said. A woman. This was news, for the golfers had told him it was a man. Sniper's bullet to the chest.

Today there were two bodies in the morgue, both at attention on the slabs. They looked very different from the living. Gloria stood by one and Brian by the other. Who were they when they were alive?

Gloria was concentrating hard. She'd got prints from the woman but there was no match. Gloria looked worried. She bit her lip. She had failed to assist, so now she doubled her efforts to identify the male. She'd get the ink prints and then attempt matches with the police database.

"How are you doing, Gloria?" Brian called across the two dead terrorists.

"OK, thanks. Yourself?"

"You know I'm good," said Brian. "I always like coming here. If I wasn't here I'd just be playing golf. That's not glamour, is it?"

"No, this is the glamour. Or at least, it's more glamorous than my general duties policing."

"How so?"

"That turned out to be a series of threats and fights – and getting dead people here to the morgue."

"You know," said Brian, "I've been watching all those TV shows about forensic clues at a crime scene and on the body. They never have a dentist. I'm just not sexy enough."

Gloria didn't know what to say about Brian being sexy. She'd been marked down on people skills, and she had sought to overcome this by working exclusively with the dead.

Brian pushed the auburn hair away from his patient's eyes and noted the disturbing blue irises. He got the plates in her mouth easily – there was no rigor yet. He noted the gold tooth. With his magnifier, he saw inscriptions in Hebrew and Arabic. He gave thanks that his patient had not been decomposing over days or weeks. He concentrated and he clicked to take the X-ray. The easy technical part was done.

Brian waved in the mortuary assistant to take down his dictation on the teeth. 'Why would a beauty like that get involved in terrorism?' mused the assistant.

Brian was not to be distracted. "I represent the dead, be they high or low, beautiful or ugly. All are equal. I give them the dignity of a name."

The coroner's sergeant came in and told Brian there was a strong lead on identification. A granny had seen the Channel 7 coverage and rung the hotline, claiming that the man front and centre on the television was her grandson Moshe. She got a glimpse of his girlfriend Leah through the window. Leah was a regular at the Central Synagogue in Bondi Junction.

Brian called the Bondi Junction dentists. The job was done and it was uncomplicated. Such satisfaction. It was the gold tooth that made it easy, then the X-rays were transmitted down the line and there was a confirmed ID. Within seconds the coroner's sergeant passed the address to the Counter Terrorism team, and cars were on the road heading east across the city.

"The granny rang back, Brian," said the sergeant. "They're bringing her in to see if she identifies our man. Her name's Rebekah."

"Does she know Leah and Moshe are both dead?" asked Brian.

"She'll soon see that this is a morgue," said the sergeant.

Brian cleaned up according to the strict protocols. He was looking forward to telling the golfers what he had done. Gloria still bit her lip as she tried to identify her man.

As Brian exited the autopsy room, he found himself face-to-face with two women. A young one in jeans and sneakers gripped the arm of an old lady wearing a black dress and shawl.

"Come on, Rebekah," the younger woman urged.

"You're not a police officer," shouted the older lady in a thick Eastern European accent. "Where is your uniform?"

Agitated and unaware of her surroundings, she banged straight into Brian's solid bulk. Brian steadied her and she fell into his arms. She seemed to find his white coat reassuring and fortunately did not look down to the bare golfer's legs beneath.

"Do you have my grandson, Doctor?"

Brian held her and she shook and mumbled – possibly in Hungarian.

"Then there was worse, Doctor," she suddenly shouted. "Golf wasn't enough. He took up philosophy." She sobbed and rocked, all the while clutching Brian. "I still prayed, Doctor, and God gave him Leah – she was almost Jewish."

A trail of spittle ran down the old lady's chin as she looked Brian in the eye. "She wasn't normal, Doctor. Her mother was Muslim, and her brother's a returned jihadi in the mental hospital." Brian hung on grimly. "But she was talking to the Rabbi, and I kept praying."

The younger woman took Rebekah by both arms and Brian was released. He was surrounded by uniforms and driven to the waiting helicopter. The rain had lightened and there was not the same urgency.

* * *

I don't like the dream. It's a big flash and I wake with a start, hot and burning. I can't fly. My wings don't work and I crash. It's pain.

Sometimes the needles. They sting. But it's Sebastian with the needle, and he rubs the spot and says it will be better.

Then he tells the long story of the sea eagle whose wing was broken. When he tells the story – I know every word, he massages my scars. Noel and he nursed the eagle - a boy eagle - and gave him fish. When Sebastian thought the feathers had grown he let the eagle go and it flew but crashed into the side of the cliff at Point Perpendicular. It couldn't fly high enough. Sebastian had to scale that cliff to get that eagle and carry it back. And after more sleeps and more fish, it flew again and made it over the mountain.

I remember when he said to me, "You, Donnie, you'll fly, and if you're not so good at first, you'll be good later. I'll be watching to make sure."

This is what I remember and this is what I dream. Sometimes it's a nightmare and sometimes it's a pleasure.

13

As the police helicopter hovered off the cliff face at Desolation Point, Brian looked out the window and saw a pelican standing in a cave mouth, next to a pile of burning wood. Sebastian stepped up to the fire and put his arm around the pelican.

Brian checked his watch. Capable as ever, he had been away just one hour. Procedure had triumphed in a world of insanity.

Donnie and Sebastian heard the all-clear siren. Donnie took off to the north and circled in a wide arc back over Desolation Point. Following her lead, Sebastian left the cave and scrambled up the steep path towards the links.

As the police helicopter landed on the soggy fourteenth tee and Brian emerged, he could see in the far distance that Stefan and the Rabbi were scurrying up Pensioners Hill.

By the time Sebastian arrived at the fourteenth tee, the air had become still and the helicopter was disappearing south. The Rabbi and Stefan were struggling in the distance like pensioners.

"She was your patient," said Brian, "and she was a she."

Brian enjoyed being direct, but Sebastian didn't really react. The truth was, these days he didn't react.

Brian continued. "She had a gold tooth with initials engraved in it, in Arabic and Hebrew."

Sebastian looked at Brian without understanding.

"Someone recognised her on Channel 7 and rang the hotline. When she waved a gun they shot her. Mad Leah."

Sebastian's mind started up and so did the horror – it was Leah. It had crossed Sebastian's mind that she might be radicalised. Zak was the confirmed head chopper, but Leah! He had dismissed the thought, and viewed her like a doctor should, not through the lens of a risk assessor. Should he have done more? Sebastian had another vision of his dead patients, coming out of a long tunnel to claim him, joined this time by Leah.

"She organised for you to be at her death scene," said Brian. "And the Rabbi."

Sebastian recalled with further horror that he had sent her to the very Rabbi who now trudged up Pensioners Hill.

"Her front man was a stooge," continued Brian. "She was directing him. And to top it off, she organised her university professor to see her die." Brian gestured towards Stefan who had slowed in his ascent of Pensioners Hill.

Sebastian felt his pulse and cursed his rejection of the pacemaker. He went to his pocket for the tablets.

Brian saw this. Could he have been more subtle with the bad news? Probably not. Why did Sebastian seem so moved by this death?

"They said it was suicide, Sebastian," said Brian, "and you might need water to swallow those tablets." He passed a flask and Sebastian took a swig, his expression still horrified. "Suicide by cop, they said. I'm so sorry."

"I didn't know she was there."

Brian had not been there himself but had the clarity of the later police analysis. "Their guns were caught by the Channel 7 camera," he said. "Then Counter Terrorism took over."

"Counter Terrorism?" echoed Sebastian, not quite taking it in.

Brian was grappling with the idea that Sebastian's view from the Paradise Motel had been so limited that he knew very little. "You heard the shots, didn't you?" he asked.

"Was there a girl at the siege? Leah?"

"Leah was in the back room, Sebastian," explained Brian, "running the show."

"I don't think she was a terrorist."

Brian saw the shadow settle over Sebastian and adopted the Irish solution of just talking away. He believed in the therapy of a good yarn. "I don't know about calling her a terrorist. My grandfather was IRA. They called him a terrorist."

As the line of suicide cases receded back into its tunnel in time with his quieting pulse, Sebastian was able to give Brian his proper attention.

"Yeah, it was a secret," said Brian. "By the time I was born the old IRA had moved up to the establishment and Finean was a superintendent in the Garda. He was only five foot five, the talking branch of the IRA, Mum said."

"The talking branch of the IRA."

"Yes, he was the talking branch of the Garda, too. Somebody has to do the talking."

"Talking branch of the Garda," repeated Sebastian.

"Like you're the talking branch of the New South Wales Police."

Sebastian's face lightened.

"And like this foursome is the talking branch of the Desolation Point Golf Links," continued Brian.

"Did you know him?" Sebastian asked.

"Not enough. He died in Spain where he thought he had sanctuary. You'd think there was safety in victory, you would, but no – they were a vicious lot. He had to run for it, in the end."

"That's sad," said Sebastian.

"He got high in the Garda because he was old IRA, the critics said, envy dripping from them. They had brains like vegetables, and in their ignorance they could not abide a good man."

"How'd you get to be six foot three then?" asked Sebastian.

"Better diet under the Republic."

"It gave you curly hair," said Sebastian.

"Didn't give me the brains, though. All I do is teeth. Mother saw teeth as an opportunity in Ireland, teeth generally being so bad at home. She thought it safe, and she didn't think the authorities would be around in the night looking for the dentist."

"She didn't think they'd be sending the police helicopter after you," observed Sebastian.

"I got to be establishment too. I play golf. Fin played the hurling." Sebastian felt himself smiling as Brian continued. "He was pleased I was a dentist and not IRA. 'Keep yourself safe,' he said, 'and you can help the police. You can ID the dead from their teeth, if they ever went to a dentist.'"

Sebastian gave silent thanks for the generosity of the Irish. He sensed the wind start to move and felt alive once more. He looked up and saw that Donnie was circling.

He had feared he would not survive another crazy death of someone he knew. Now it was upon him.

Still, who better with a death message than Brian? He could talk down an impacted wisdom tooth without even the threat of a needle.

Firm in his conviction that Brian was a talented therapist, Sebastian tried to explain his feelings. He started with his recent experience in the hermit's cave. "Such communication, Brian. All without words."

"But you can talk to him."

"Yes, I can talk to Noel a little bit. I meant Donnie, she says nothing."

"I see," said Brian. "Does it matter?"

"No, it doesn't matter. All those words at the siege, Brian, quite sophisticated it was, substantial talk of philosophy and theology, God and the whole shebang."

"That sort of talk was never going to help," said Brian.

"Yes, and then it's all resolved with a gun. And I think I'm turning into a zombie."

"No, Sebastian, you're not a zombie."

"It's been a close thing. I've been saved by the pelican, and the hermit. And the mates. And the golf."

"I didn't think you were even close," said Brian. "We've got plenty of zombies here at Desolation Point – but I never thought you were one of them."

"I am close, Brian. I could become a very efficient zombie engaged professionally in the smooth running of society. A zombie could do the deaths, suicides, inquests, police sieges and all that sort of thing. Zombies carry less risk for society. It's real humans that cause all the trouble."

Brian paused. "I can only say, Sebastian, that it's important to have a bit of fun. Even at the morgue, I can have a bit of fun. That forensics girl Gloria, trying to get the fingerprints from the deceased, she's a real hoot."

Sebastian understood that the misery weighed the dentist down, and admired Brian's lightness.

"It doesn't have to be all depressing," Brian said. "The misery brings out the best in some of us. Like Finean, from IRA to the Garda, and still enjoying a bit of the crack all the way, even when he was persecuted by people with vegetables for brains and vitriol in their juices."

"For me it's the bird – Donnie," said Sebastian. "I think to myself, Donnie, you're injured but still flying. And even though the words are lacking, the communication is like a diamond."

"I don't really know the bird," said Brian, "but obviously she's a total champion."

Sebastian looked up and pointed. "There she is again," he said. "She appeared when I arrived, when I got back from the siege and when I checked on the hermit. Now, when the worst of it all is revealed, there she is again."

"That's a big day for a pelican," said Brian. "Why is it that this pelican is so close?"

"It's Noel's instruction," said Sebastian. "He's sending her out."

"I don't really know about Noel," said Brian. "I don't know how to separate the myth from the man."

"He doesn't want any myth, he just wants for people to stop talking and to be left alone."

"I didn't mean he wanted myth," said Brian, "but the myth has come from somewhere."

"He hardly even talks to me. He says he's renounced talk. The talk interferes with his communication with the bird. And his appreciation of beauty."

"I saw from the helicopter, Sebastian. He's got the beauty."

Sebastian and Brian fell silent, watching the bird, gazing out and engaging with the beauty.

With Stefan trailing, the Rabbi breathlessly approached them. "Well, who was he?" he called.

* * *

I'm alive. Some say it's instinct, survival instinct. I don't know.

Because of Noel's help and Sebastian's help, I live. I can fly, not like I once did, but quite good for an old girl. I met another pelican and I had my babies, all since the scarring.

Damage means death around here. The hawks get the lame rabbits. The injured ducklings don't last long.

I don't like the big black bird, and I don't like the police with their guns. Sebastian said it was necessary because there were others with guns. Some just wanted to kill living things and he reminded me of the unhinged gunman shooting pelicans years ago at Point Perpendicular.

14

The Rabbi waved his arms about as he spoke animatedly with Brian. Donnie hovered above. A family of small rabbits put their heads up out of the long grass and watched intently. So did Stefan as he recovered his breath. And so did Sebastian.

When the Rabbi learned that a woman had been shot by the police, he was surprised. "But it was a man I spoke with, a man with tatts. Tatts about the Maccabiah Games. I know him. He was a golfer."

"He was just a stooge," said Brian. "The woman was inside directing him." He had the Rabbi's full attention.

"Well, who was she?"

"Mad Leah," said Brian.

"But...but?"

"I just ID'ed her at the morgue. She had distinctive dental work."

"Explain it to me, Brian. Please."

"She organised to have you there," said Brian, reciting the police talk. "She wanted to die in front of you."

Sebastian butted in. "I didn't think she was violent."

"Nor did I," said the Rabbi. "She was such a sweet girl, and she liked you, Sebastian. Yes she did, she saw you as the hope for her brother and herself."

"What did she say?" asked Sebastian.

"That you were helping her in her confusion and telling her to come to the synagogue."

"I was happy about that – better than online instruction in jihadism."

The Rabbi continued to wave his arms about, and the rabbits continued to watch him.

"I told her that her background didn't have to make it all tragic."

"What?"

"Her crazy background. Her father married outside the faith," said the Rabbi. "Baghdad was tolerant once upon a time, but the family got persecution from the new fundamentalists."

The Rabbi appeared to calm down as he explained Leah's background. His arms dropped to his sides. "She thought the solution was to make herself Jewish – officially, totally Jewish."

"Did she have to convince you to let her in?" asked Sebastian.

"We were working our way through it."

"She never talked suicide," said Sebastian.

The Rabbi shrunk to a smaller and more contained unit. "No, she did not," he said. "And yet she's done it."

As the Rabbi became more sombre, Stefan pressed forward. "That front man certainly talked a lot of rubbish. I couldn't see the point, and it turns out there was no point, except to get us there and keep us there."

"They were both your students," said Brian. "Apparently they met doing your philosophy course in death and euthanasia, it was a common interest."

Stefan gaped at Brian.

Brian continued with the bleak narrative. "The report said Channel 7 caught the guns. Then there was the stun grenade and the dog went in with a camera, and the men in black knew exactly what they were dealing with when a sniper shot your two students. You heard the shots, didn't you?"

Still Stefan did not react, and nor did the Rabbi.

"I've told you what I know," said Brian. "I only know what they told me at the morgue. I'm only the dentist."

The Rabbi was starting to get it. What do I do? he thought. That poor girl. I've been played for a shmuck. Couldn't they just shoot her in the leg?

Why did she get me there? And why did they take me away? He needed to be telling Esther this stuff, as he did at the end of each day. But here he was on the golf course, with his psychiatrist and philosopher, and a dentist. He still had his toothache but he wasn't sure he could go to Brian, now that Brian had been inside Leah's dead mouth.

The Rabbi didn't know what else to do, so he tried to stroke his drive from the fourteenth tee. He failed completely on the weight transfer. His ball faded abruptly in the wind and sailed right over the cliff to the beach below. It could not be recovered. Things were getting worse.

He tried to imagine what Esther would say, then he tried prayer, but he couldn't connect. Because he was admiring what he took to be Sebastian's calm in a crisis, he decided to try psychiatry.

"Penny for your thoughts?" he said, but Sebastian was at that moment focusing on Donnie, circling high above.

"I'm looking at Donnie," he said, and the Rabbi was not impressed. "She stops me thinking about all my deceased patients," explained Sebastian.

Brian hit from the tee. "Good hit," he said of his own shot. "As good as a good one."

Nobody knew what this meant. It was complex, unlike Brian. But they were all well used to him and put it down as Irish.

"I envy you, Rabbi," said Sebastian, as his suicide cases again came out of the tunnel and circled him. "You get to do these eulogies, and then the dead are laid to rest. I wish I could lay my dead to rest like that."

The Rabbi had made a mistake in turning to the psychiatrist on this particular occasion. He turned to the dentist. "I've never heard of anyone having their initials on their teeth," he said.

"They do it all the time. When the gold is melted it's lovely to work with, and you can put whatever you want on the teeth. One of my patients had the map of Ireland."

Sebastian was on the tee. What the hell? *There's no pleasure in the safe shot.* I don't have time left to waste like that. I'll try a real shot. He swung from inside to out, followed through extravagantly, turned his wrists, and moved the ball fifty metres right to left, and two hundred metres down the fairway, with overspin.

The Rabbi was still looking at him as Donnie flew past with a wing tilt and Brian said, "Good hit. As good as a good one."

In the ugly face of all the objective evidence, I still have belief, thought Sebastian. Is it faith, or is it insanity?

He saw that Stefan, still gaping, had followed his ball's majestic flight. "I can do it Stefan," he called.

"Why is it that you only come alive in an impossible situation?" retorted Stefan.

"All my life," said Sebastian, "it's backs to the wall, the impossible, the hopeless challenge, the contest going the wrong way. It's into the gale, psychiatrically the lost cause. I am the bush lawyer, I argue the impossible. I undertake to treat the terminally crippled."

"What would your patients say if they knew the truth?"

"Indeed. I'm mad. A crazed Don Quixote, modelling the transformation. Ha ha ha."

"You look like a patient with your wild wind-blown hair."

"Why thank you, Stefan. That's lovely of you. And you too look like a patient in your wet baggy shorts and your funny hat."

"Thank you," said Stefan. "At least my head is dry. But why, Sebastian? Why? Why always the lost causes?"

"Well basically that's it, isn't it? The cause is lost, we are all fucked and those who can accept this truth turn me on slightly. I guess I respond a teensy bit, within the limits imposed by decorum. They select me, I select them."

Stefan teed his ball but could not get himself comfortable. "I have the usual dilemma of whether to try harder or to relax."

"Give up," called Sebastian. "Give up entirely and you may be redeemed."

"Right. Should be easy," mumbled Stefan, and then hit his own boomer, straight and true, fading slightly into the southerly, such that the wind held it in balance and dropped it softly into prime position.

"See," said Sebastian.

"Great shot. How did you do that?" asked the Rabbi.

"I gave up all hope, on Sebastian's advice." Stefan looked at Sebastian. "If you know what to do, how come you're such a bad golfer?"

"I'm only human."

"And do you consider you are a good psychiatrist?"

"Being human helps. Making mistakes is very important. It gives me a lot of credibility. People don't want perfect doctors who don't make mistakes. They are a pain in the ass."

"It is in the nature of things that they fall apart," said Stefan.

"Yes, yes." Sebastian was getting excited, as he often did in the wind. "And people understand this. They know they're not on a winner, we all die and we all suffer. They are prepared to cut their shrink some slack, they don't demand a perfect result. I ask you this. What are the odds on a perfect result? About the same as the odds on you returning a par round. Miracles happen but they are brief and then they are followed by reality. That's what we've got – we're signed up to it. Unless we get psychotic."

Donnie came from the clouds and flew low over Sebastian's head with an extravagant wing tilt.

As they came down the fourteenth, the weather didn't know what to do. The headland was clouded but the sun came through overhead. The wind blew gusts, then flurries, then stilled, then started from the other side.

"I remember you when you had hope and idealism," said Stefan. "You were against the Establishment."

"I do remember outrage," said Sebastian. "But it faded with my professional development. I had to fit the mould, even if suppressing what I held dear."

"What was that?" asked Stefan.

"I don't really remember now, the memory faded with the outrage. What I do remember is I had to fit myself into a pinstripe suit and everyone gawked at me. It was ludicrous, just like the belief system I had to adopt."

"And that was?"

"I had to be highly trained, relied on in an emergency to do much the same as somebody else with the same training. 'Trained' was the word – like a dog."

"But what then?" asked Stefan. "Did you not keep your own private system?"

"I don't remember, although I did toy with the idea of blowing up Ward Two at Callan Park."

"Yeah, I remember that. We were reassured. And now it's reopened as an assessment centre for returned jihadis, with you as the chief assessor."

"So it goes," said Sebastian.

"At least you get to influence something," said Stefan. "I don't. Totally private I am, even though I keep writing in the academic journals. Nobody ever responds. They think I'm weird."

"We're both weird," said Sebastian.

He pointed to the Rabbi, who trudged down the left side of the fairway, where his second attempt from the tee had finished. "It's the Rabbi we rely on. Basically you and I are unstable."

The wind picked up and briefly Sebastian had a lift but soon it fell and he dropped with it. "The Rabbi brings me back to reality," he said. "He's my anchor. When it's just you and me, we start talking about phantoms, what we really believe or used to believe, or think we remember about it."

"I'm often on my own anyway, without either of you. Nobody ever responds to my inner thoughts when I write them in the philosophy journals. So what's the point?"

Donnie flew overhead as Sebastian addressed his ball, broad wings flapping rhythmically but with obvious effort. "Look," he said, "it's windless. I can't think when it's like this, and even for Donnie it's an effort to get anywhere. How am I supposed to play golf?"

"Go back to your training," suggested Stefan. "Stick to the essentials, the basics."

"I didn't have basic training, except in how to steal golf balls and how to run away from the greenkeeper. Now I just lurch about from one extreme to another."

"Yes, so they say."

"Who says?"

"The golfers in the clubhouse think you're nuts. The other day they showed me the scatter on your scorecard. You carded every possible score between two and eight. 'Wild,' they said, 'undisciplined. Talented but what a shame. Unpredictable.'"

"You know it depends on the wind. When it blows, I'm good. And I'm not into trying hard just to make things look good. That's my day job."

"At least they talk to you in your day job, they don't talk to me."

"I wish," said Sebastian. "I could do without the vituperation. It varies. They don't all talk tough, some just look at me, and I wish they wouldn't. But I have to keep myself nice. If I were as wild as them, the situation would be inflammatory."

"Is there much wind at Callan Park?" asked Stefan.

"No, that's part of the problem. I'd function much better on a headland, in a seaside mental hospital."

Sebastian imagined his next encounter with Zak. How would he break the news that Leah was dead?

What sense could there possibly be? Zak would be alone, without family, trust or hope.

"Any birdlife at Callan Park?" asked Stefan.

"No. It's very sad in that department."

A mother duck crossed Sebastian's path and he watched patiently. She was followed by seven ducklings, and at the end of the line, a father duck. They all stopped from time to time, and pecked at the ground for grubs and beetles. Sebastian waited until they passed into the long grass, and he continued his journey.

* * *

Sebastian healed me and he keeps working on Noel. But I see him fiddle with his bracelet and I see him take his pills.

When the rain falls the other golfers go off the links. But Sebastian doesn't stop. He keeps going.

15

The fourteenth at Desolation Point was known as *The Clifftop* and the fifteenth was known as *The Precipice*. For Sebastian these were the hardest holes in the entirety of the links, which he now privately thought of as *The Desolation*.

The ragged foursome had hit from the fourteenth tee and approached the clifftop green. Stefan and Sebastian walked together. They were on top of their world, with nothing above them. To the south there was Point Horizontal and to the north, Point Perpendicular. The reef lay five hundred metres offshore. Six pelicans were enjoying the updrafts, soaring up from below the golfers and appearing in their eye line as they tried to focus on their shots.

When the pelicans soared up and over the edge of the precipice, they locked eyes with Sebastian. Once, he had flown with them.

A lifetime ago, Noel had found the broken hang-glider at the base of the cliff, where it was smashed up by rocks and surf. He repaired the glider with his second-hand fibreglass kit. He said it would be good for his golf, to get up there and be in the wind. He said he would come to know what the birds knew.

The first step for Sebastian was the leap of faith. It had been OK to jump in the deep end at the rock pool. Then it was OK to jump into the Warriewood blowhole when the waves were running. Leaping off Point Desolation seemed a bigger call. It was a three hundred metre drop and the smashed glider had been at the bottom.

Noel, however, was of a different mind. "Don't think about it," he said, as he ran straight off the precipice with his arms outstretched. As Sebastian watched, Noel was taken by the updraft and lifted to another realm. He spiralled and banked, he caught a following wind along the precipice, on which he swept, chased and arced. Eventually he stalled and without grace crashed in a deep bunker guarding the fifteenth green.

"Have a go," Noel said, spitting wet sand from his mouth, and Sebastian's life changed.

Surfing had been one thing. It was the moment of being taken by the wave that thrilled Sebastian.

When he went to the men's barber and read about sex, the descriptions in the magazines aligned it with surfing. At that special moment, control was all gone. When he went off Point Desolation on the glider, it was a rolling orgasm. There was no thinking, he was lifted and he was gone. On his left a pelican, on his right a pelican. He felt he had arrived at his destination, or he was taken to it. He was the Prince of Point Desolation.

Later, when he could think a little straighter, and had some experience of life, he preferred sex after all. When he crashed the glider, he found that pain actually hurt, and he lost his courage. Noel never did prefer sex, and he continued for a time to fly with the pelicans, to crash, and to repair the beast where it was kept in the caves below the fourteenth tee.

So now when the pelicans came and locked their eyes with his, Sebastian wished still that he could fly but knew he could not. Under his breath, he said, "I envy you. I've learned from you and I've taken. I thought I was better. And now, my golf in the wind – a sad imitation of you, glorious pelican." Yet, in the wind with Donnie, he was suspended on a magic thread connecting earth and heaven.

"Why do you do these dangerous things?" asked Stefan suddenly. "Like police sieges?"

"I gave up hang-gliding," replied Sebastian, shifting his attention from the birds.

"Be serious, Sebastian. You said you can't stand another death. Why work with jihadis and police sieges?"

"I was irrelevant. I wanted to be back in public life. And it was exciting."

"You always got bored easily."

"Yeah, and I thought police psychiatry would be challenging in my later years."

"You used not to like police," said Stefan.

"But I found we have something in common. They remove people from society, so do I. Bad or mad, the difference is not always clear."

"But the death, Sebastian. I don't know how you cope with so many deaths."

This too was a tough question. "It's the golf – somehow things are bigger out here in the desolation." He paused. "And it's the mates. I'm fond of some of you."

In reality, it surprised Sebastian that the foursome coped at all. Two deaths and still they were maintaining the pace of play at Desolation Point. When all else failed, one put one's foot in front of one's other foot. One hit the ball, walked after it and hit it again.

"In all the eccentricities of the day," said Sebastian, "our golf is reasonably normal. We had a beginning, we continued and despite everything, we persevered."

"We did," said the Rabbi, joining them on the green.

"They gave no indication," said Stefan. "I couldn't do anything because they didn't say anything."

"So? Isn't that the way it goes?" said Sebastian.

"I should have done something," said the Rabbi.

Stefan startled. "I remember now, his semester paper – *The Morality of Suicide*. He even wrote about terrorist bombers and suicide by cop."

"How could you forget?" said Sebastian.

"I gave him a fail. I told him it was outside the guidelines of the essay question."

"No," said the Rabbi.

"His girlfriend became angry with me," said Stefan.

"No," said the Rabbi again, "surely not. Not a paper on *Suicide by Cop*?"

The foursome went silent as they completed their putting at *The Clifftop* and recorded their scores. The pelicans continued to soar in the updraft as the surf churned against the reef and the waves crashed at the base of the cliff below.

* * *

I was busy from the time the big black bird returned and the tall one got out. He was OK but soon the fat one was waving his arms, the bald one was changing his face again, and even Sebastian changed his colour. I had to watch closely.

16

They stood at the fifteenth tee at Desolation Point, known as *The Precipice*.

"Sebastian, do you think I'm normal?" asked Stefan.

"Stefan, you are about four standard deviations from the mean score on all the key indicators. You're off the graph."

"But do you think I can be normal?"

"No. Now stop this nonsense and hit the golf ball."

"I don't think he's that bad," said the Rabbi.

"Yes, he is," said Sebastian. "I'm the psychiatrist, and he's the worst of the worst."

"Hang on," said the Rabbi.

"You're just being all pastoral, Rabbi. He's bad. It's time to call it out."

"No, he's not that bad, it's just that he's honest," said the Rabbi. "Most people aren't honest about themselves like Stefan."

"Well, thank God for that," said Sebastian. "What sort of life would I have if everybody went on about themselves like he did?"

Stefan looked from Sebastian to the Rabbi and back again. "Is there no hope for me?"

"There's always hope," said the Rabbi.

"There's no hope," said Sebastian. "Your best bet is to give up hope."

"Every time I come here to Desolation Point, I have hope. I want to be a normal golfer," said Stefan. "I look at that sign on the first tee *Hope*, and I think, yeah, I've got it."

"It could have been called *The Illusion of Hope*," said Sebastian, "but there was insufficient room on the plate to write all that, according to the engraver."

"But Sebastian, I'm more normal than these people of yours who have been shot by police." Stefan smiled at what he had said, and with that he teed his ball and hit with decisiveness and without the usual preliminaries.

"Good quick shot," said Sebastian.

"Bobby-dazzler," said Brian.

"What's got into you?" exclaimed the Rabbi.

"Normality," said Stefan. "I may be unusual, but I'm getting normal."

"You'll find it lonely," said Sebastian.

"I'll be alive," said Stefan. "Unlike your patient."

"Hang on," said the Rabbi again.

"His patient is dead," said Stefan. "That's a lot of standard deviations away from being alive."

"I'll have to think about that," said the Rabbi.

"And this terrorist golfer of yours – he's dead too, absolutely not alive."

"Well, you were teaching him all that stuff on suicide and euthanasia," said the Rabbi.

"I didn't teach him much," replied Stefan.

"Just enough apparently," said Sebastian.

"He could have just killed himself. He didn't have to put me in danger, or the Rabbi."

"He needed me there," said the Rabbi. "He needed closure on the whole sad thing. I didn't say before."

"What?" asked Sebastian, relieved the Rabbi was finally coming clean.

"He talked about Leah and how she wasn't going to make it. She was suicidal, he said, despite being gorgeous."

"Yes, she was a gorgeous girl," said Stefan. "I wondered why she was with that older guy, with all the tatts. But when she got angry, boy, did she get angry."

"Yes, angry enough to get herself and her boyfriend killed," said the Rabbi.

"Yes," said Sebastian. "She was angry. Her brother cut heads off infidels, but he seemed a mild-mannered sort at the hospital compared to her – quite nice when he wasn't killing. Leah got crazy mad when the nurse wouldn't let him have his cigarettes. I could see the potential."

"I never saw her angry," said the Rabbi. "Not that she was all sweetness and light. Actually quite dark, when she got going on her family and Baghdad."

"She was mad as hell when I gave the boyfriend a fail," said Stefan. "What right did I have to fail him, she yelled. Discrimination, she called it. It's not discrimination, I said, it's just that he didn't answer the essay question – *The Morality of Suicide*. He wrote about terrorist bombers and suicide by cop. She was mad and he just looked at me like a zombie. I called security."

"Yes, he got zombie-like in the end," said the Rabbi. "Good golfer. Maybe a bit fanatical, but how do you pick a real fanatic from a group of golfers? It went bad for him after the bridge collapsed. He got sick and couldn't play."

"Do you know how they met?" asked Sebastian. "I only knew Leah. I didn't know Moshe at all."

"I never saw them together," said the Rabbi. "Leah was coming to see me, but I hadn't seen Moshe for years. I wouldn't have thought them a good match anyway."

"How do you know that?" asked Sebastian.

"I ran singles groups for years, with Esther. I had a very high success rate on matchmaking. My mother said it was my gift."

"So it must have been me," said Stefan. "I remember now. A particular tutorial on terrorism. Everybody had gone, but there they were, eyes lighting up on suicide and terrorism. Then she was tracing over all his tatts, with her fingers. And they caught me looking. I felt such a goat."

"So," said Brian, "you did it, Stefan. Put the two terrorists together. What a match. Me, I met my wife at a dance."

"I admit a mistake," said Stefan. "I should not have failed him on his essay. He may have been trying to tell me something. OK, I made a mistake calling security when she said I was discriminating against him with a fail. Maybe she had a point. I didn't listen. But I didn't know she was going to do a full-on terrorist act, with a police siege and everything, and involve the lot of us.'

Stefan appealed to them. "You're supposed to know these things, Rabbi. Why didn't you listen to her? All that time counselling or whatever. And you, Sebastian. Why didn't you do something? You could have locked her up. Told Counter Terrorism about her. Don't you know an angry terrorist when they're right in front of you?"

Sebastian was holding his driving club quite tightly as Stefan spoke. He had a quick image of a blow to the right temple, then Stefan was on the ground and red blood was running across the green grass. He was distracted by the same family of ducks – mother, seven ducklings, father duck – as they continued their waddling march, crossing the fifteenth green and back towards the tee where they would commence their long descent to the low country and the large dam where they surely would resume swimming lessons. He worried for them being so far from home. They had done well to climb Pensioners Hill, when it had been such an effort for others.

"You think I'm four standard deviations off the mean, what about you? You're a psychiatrist. That puts you a few standard deviations out. Even compared to other shrinks, you're a few standard deviations out. Other shrinks don't ride around in police helicopters."

Sebastian had lost contact with the family of ducks but was still trying to play golf, despite the head noises. Now there were some extra noises, coming from Stefan. As usual when the line of deceased patients came out of the tunnel and encircled him, his concentration was stretched. Look at the dot on the back of the ball, the Rabbi always said, and he tried that. But he always had trouble with his drive when there was a ghoulish gallery focused upon him.

"I admit everything," said Sebastian in a loud voice, as though projecting widely. "I'm crazy. Absolutely – just like Stefan. And I'm quite sure my craziness has an impairing effect on performance. And I'd like to apologise for all future mistakes. I'm sorry."

The Rabbi and Brian had turned to listen to Sebastian's announcement.

"You're not that bad," said Brian.

"I'd be worse if not for you, Brian."

"I agree," said the Rabbi, "you're not so bad."

"Rabbi, it's you who holds me up, just like you hold him up." He pointed at Stefan, who was rummaging in his bag for a sandwich. "I could be worse, and I never said I was perfect. In fact, I've often fessed up to being crazy."

"Yes," said the Rabbi. "It gives you charm."

"Yes," said Brian, "it's good for the talk. And without the talk, where would we be?"

"Guys, we've stopped playing," said Sebastian. "We're standing here at the height of Desolation Point arguing. The group behind wants us to keep moving. We don't get to stop our progress without a very good reason. I'm hitting."

Sebastian hit his ball without delay or preliminaries. It soared confidently.

"A ripsnorter," called Brian.

"Bobby-dazzler," called the Rabbi.

"Next," called Sebastian.

"Me. I'm good to go," said Brian. "I had nothing to do with either of them until I met them at the morgue. No trauma for me, I'm good to go."

And Brian, the quickest of the four, hit straight off the cliff of *The Precipice*, knowing the updraft would catch the ball and hold it and return it to the fairway.

"As good as a good one," called Sebastian.

"At least as good as a good one," called the Rabbi.

"That makes no sense to a philosopher, it's not logical," said Stefan.

"Next," called Sebastian.

The Rabbi teed up and hit without reflection, over the waves. His ball suspended itself on the wind, and as it did so, the Rabbi said, "I don't mind death. I guess it doesn't count against me. It's part of my normal routine. I'm the death man."

Time seemed to stop as the Rabbi spoke and while they all tried to think of a reply, Donnie came downwind from the reef and passed the Rabbi's ball, which veered and followed Donnie across the cliff face and on to the safety of the cut grass. The Rabbi's ball had followed the very trajectory of Noel's ball in the final round of the Australian Open in 1967. Then it was Noel who trusted and hit out over the waves. He was five strokes down with just four holes to play, and it was here that he started his charge to victory.

"Well played," said Sebastian, hauling himself back from 1967.

"Rabbi," said Stefan, "I spend all my time on death too."

"Yeah, but you're an intellectual and you've got young intellectual students," said the Rabbi. "What have I got? Dead people and their grieving relatives."

"Is this good?"

"No but it's my life – circumcisions and funerals."

"What about his funeral?" asked Sebastian.

"Yeah, he didn't actually kill himself. I'm prepared to do the funeral, as he asked. It was important to him. Apparently I made a difference once, when he was a kid, in the golf team."

"He didn't need to drag me along to get closure," said Stefan.

"Well," said the Rabbi, "he said you were a bit theoretical and should see a real angry suicide."

"He's right, and he's done me good."

"What about my funeral?" asked Sebastian.

"You're not dead," replied the Rabbi.

"I'm close. I want a booking."

"OK. You're in."

"Thank you. What about Leah?"

"OK. She's in too."

The Rabbi set off from the tee followed by the others but he stopped abruptly. The foursome stood together as another family of ducks crossed in front of the fifteenth tee, towards the precipice. The mother duck put her head in the air and looked first at the golfers then at the offshore reef. She turned in a wide waddle and was followed by her seven ducklings and the father duck. The Rabbi nodded his approval and then proceeded alongside the precipice.

* * *

The fat one stopped waving in the end. Sebastian kept looking up to find me. He pointed and the others looked up too. They all shouted a bit and they stopped playing. It looked like there was going to be a fight. It was all worse than a big storm with lightning.

The tall one kept smiling. In the end the fat one hit the ball and it soared out over the ocean. I took off after it and it curved back on the wind and landed on the grass. He was OK after that, for a while. He smiled at the ducklings.

17

As Sebastian stood on the sixteenth tee, his eyes were again cast up to Donnie flying in her wide spirals. The sixteenth hole was known as *Acceptance*. He paid attention only to Donnie.

"Did you see where my ball went?" called the Rabbi.

Stefan had been getting another sandwich out of his bag, although he had promised not to eat in front of the Rabbi during his strict diet. "Sorry, I was getting my water bottle. It's the heat." It came out muffled because he was trying to chew his sandwich unnoticed.

The Rabbi turned to Sebastian. "You've been watching Donnie again, haven't you?"

Sebastian was still in his reverie.

"Well, you have, haven't you?" shouted the Rabbi.

"Yes, Rabbi," he confessed solemnly.

"My ball," yelled the Rabbi, flustered and irritable. "I'm up today, first time in years, and neither of you watched. It'll be lost and I'll cop a two stroke penalty. You and your pelican. Him with his sandwich."

"Water bottle," said Stefan, again with his mouth full.

"It's a sandwich. It's in your hand behind your back."

"Sorry, Rabbi," said Sebastian. "But I do know where to look for it. I think we can find it."

The Rabbi seemed soothed. "Where would you look?"

"I heard your shot. Slightly pingy, it was. A fair strike but with a slight top edge. You've gone high, that's why you didn't see anything. It'll be coming down with snow on it. And you always fade it when you're cross about the wind. You'll be over amongst the dandelions."

"Remind me to play with someone else," said the Rabbi. He shook his head and wondered what to tell Esther.

Sebastian took his turn and teed his ball. He noted that Donnie was just twenty metres above him, banking into a north-easterly, right wing down at fifteen degrees. He knew she was coaching him, and he took the two iron to go under the wind. "You know," he announced, "pelicans are said to feed their own blood to their babies when necessary.

They wound themselves with their bill and draw the blood. That's why they are a Christ symbol."

"Hit the ball," barked the Rabbi.

Sebastian imagined Donnie's babies and wondered if Donnie thought about them.

"Good hit," said the Rabbi, who had regained his composure and Sebastian realised that he had indeed hit his ball. "Come show me where my ball is."

Sebastian limped from the sixteenth tee, as ever the high point of his day, and knew it was now the downhill path with the wind hovering.

As the golfers walked away from the long grass and dandelions where the Rabbi's ball had remained hiding, the Rabbi was stern. "I'm worried about you, Sebastian. I don't think you and Donnie are realistic."

Sebastian wondered if Esther had put him up to it. *She's probably sick and tired of the Rabbi's long reports about Donnie.* He pretends not to know Donnie when he's at Desolation Point and then when he gets home to Esther it all comes pouring out.

"What do you mean by realistic?" asked Sebastian, who in his day job often told other people they were not realistic. He thought the Rabbi was cross because his ball was lost and Sebastian's ball was sitting nicely pin-high on the sixteenth green.

Donnie came down and hovered ten metres above the Rabbi's head as they continued their downward path to the sixteenth green. Sebastian looked from one to the other. "She's realistic," he said. "Look at her."

The Rabbi was fixed on Sebastian, unable to look up.

"Stefan, is there a pelican over the Rabbi's head?"

Stefan looked from the Rabbi to Donnie and back to Sebastian, all the while ransacking his mind for philosophical ideas about direct realism, idealism, phenomenalism and constructivism. He scratched his head. "Certainly looks like a pelican! Yeah, I'm prepared to say it's a pelican."

The Rabbi ignored Stefan. "Sebastian, you are the only golfer at Desolation Point claiming to be coached by a pelican. You may be delusional." The Rabbi had worried about Sebastian since his mother's ashes went up into the pelican spirals over the sixteenth tee, then worried more when Sebastian had claimed to be in the mind of the pelican. He had spoken with Esther at length. She had pressed him for details. How close was she? Did she do the wing tilt? Did she look at him? You have to say something, she had said at breakfast, it may not be healthy to be that close with the pelican.

"You think I'm delusional?" asked Sebastian, holding the flagstick at the sixteenth and waiting for Stefan to putt, a laborious process.

"You may just be in grief, and Donnie may be ordinary, like a pigeon."

"Pigeon!" exclaimed Sebastian.

"Ah!" shouted Stefan painfully, as his putt scooted by the hole, onto the downslope and off the green altogether. "Will you shut up about pelicans and pigeons?"

"I didn't bring it up," said Sebastian.

"Sebastian," continued the Rabbi, resuming his less confrontational and more avuncular style, "maybe you're enticed. The bird may be average and not at all powerful."

Donnie looked down once more and then with a beat of her powerful wings and a tilt to the left, took off southwards into the shifting wind.

"Thank God she's gone," said Stefan, who had rummaged in his bag for the lob wedge and was approaching his ball. "Now I can have silence to play the lob wedge. I hate the lob wedge."

The little willie wagtail saw an opportunity and came up to Stefan, but failed to distract him. "Anyway," he said, "what is it that makes you think you have a special relationship with birds?"

"I don't," said Sebastian, "only a fool would think that." He gestured to the ducks in the pond behind the green. "These ducks, I'm not with them at all. I don't like the hawks, and the crows are just steely cold. It's only Donnie that I get!" The little wagtail turned from Stefan and went hopping and dancing over the green until it reached Sebastian's left foot and stood next to it.

There was a time when Sebastian may have felt like a dictator deposed from his realm of reality. But now he didn't care. "What's so good about reality anyway?" he asked the Rabbi, who looked around hopefully, wanting to resurrect in his thoughts what Esther had said at breakfast. "Reality's pretty grim," continued Sebastian. "I thought you were here to get away from it. What possible reality is there at Desolation Point?"

Stefan hit his lob wedge poorly – a difficult piece of equipment. The Rabbi's putt curled away sadly from the target.

Only two holes to go.

"I feel like giving up," announced Stefan again.

For years Sebastian had wished that he, too, could just give up, but there was always his obsessive determination in the way. He'd tried Tibetan yoga, Hindu breath control and contemplative prayer. They hadn't worked and whenever he counselled himself not to try so hard, he would try harder. It was only in his mature years and in the wind at Desolation Point that he could give up at all. He thought of it as wind meditation and giving up to the wind.

Stefan had never helped. Whenever Stefan said, "Ah, the best thing is to just give up," Sebastian knew Stefan would then be having daily golf lessons. And whenever he said, "As long as I'm suicidal I think I can get through," Sebastian knew what the philosopher meant and stayed steadfast, because he was the only one left who could handle Stefan's suicidal talk.

* * *

They started heading down from the peak and still they had to cover the low ground to get back to where they started. The wind came in fits and starts and went backwards and forwards – I don't like that. I could see Sebastian didn't like it, and the others got weird again. They shouted. I wanted to be close to Sebastian and I hovered over his head. They pointed at me and argued. I just hovered and they stopped. They continued as though they'd opened a gate and everything was different. I relaxed and went off on the wind.

18

Walking onto the seventeenth, known as *Homeward,* Stefan drifted again from suicide to death generally. "Just tip me over the cliff if I die," he said. "But what about you? Is it okay if we just tip you over? It's such a long way to carry you back to the clubhouse."

Sebastian knew the mad philosopher was merely trying to fill a gap in the conversation with philosopher's small talk. But his thoughts carried him back and down, over the stretch of sand that held Point Desolation in communion with Point Horizontal, past the pair of hawks hovering in the wind, eyes riveted to something in the long grass. His thoughts took him down by the cliffs to where the pelicans played in the updrafts, the same updrafts that carried his mother.

Let the wind take me, Sebastian thought, as he stood upon the seventeenth tee. The same tee where Noel had hit his famous one iron in 1967, to go under the powerful southerly which had defeated his high flying opponents. The links golfer can fight or give up to the wind, which is an enemy and a friend. Into the wind you hit low, under the wind. With a following wind you hit high, to get the assistance. If the wind is right to left, you can bend it left to right, to nullify – or in the alternative, aim way right.

Sebastian aimed way right, to give the ball up to the wind of the moment. What a shame Mother was frightened, and what a shame I didn't know. The birds had wanted to join in with the ashes, at least the fearless hawks and the pelicans. The hawks displayed all the skills the links golfer dreams about: resolute under the wind, speedy with the wind, banking. The pelicans did the same, but in a friendlier manner. They did not hunt while they flew.

He hit right and the wind carried his ball and delivered it. He turned to Stefan. "You'll have to carry me back to the clubhouse, because I'm needed for my funeral – so is the Rabbi."

"Fair enough but it's a long way back," said Stefan, "and it's going to be tough picking you up again every time we've played a shot."

Is this man comic or tragic? I just don't know. But if one does not seem to work there may be call for the other. "Thank you," said Sebastian, "and I'll tell the Rabbi to thank you in my eulogy."

* * *

Turning for home with what was now a following southerly, Sebastian remembered that the same southerly had appeared to carry Noel home in 1967.

Sebastian stood upon the eighteenth tee and surveyed the hole, known to the members as *Survival*. Then he did his checks. Donnie? On her tower by the eighteenth green, almost 400 metres away, facing into more dark clouds, another storm. Sebastian gave thanks again for his distance vision.

Wind direction? Exactly the opposite of the way Donnie directed her bill.

Velocity? From her posture, a three club wind.

Psychological check? Still in touch, smelling the storm and able to front death while still laughing. Detailed review on hold.

The Rabbi was organising his bag, as always when worried. It was the storm and the difficult funeral at four o'clock. First he had to get petrol, and he'd use the stop for a coke and a chocolate. Then the Holocaust survivor, a triumph of life.

He'd do justice and honour, and he'd add it to his other Holocaust eulogies. One day he'd publish and that would be his statement for life.

Stefan was still on the seventeenth mentally, although his body paced the eighteenth tee. What was now downwind had been crosswind then, and it was complicated. He had read *Zen Golf*, as well as having two more lessons, but he struggled with the Zen part. Do not try, it said, but he still tried, sometimes quite hard. There was a chapter on not aiming at the target. But as he stood behind his ball and with one eye closed, lining it up with the flag in the middle distance, he berated himself again. I need an eagle now to make B-grade. I'll never make B-grade. I just want to make B-grade before I die.

Brian gave thanks that he was no longer at the morgue identifying a dead terrorist by her teeth. He was on the lookout for lightning and saw the clouds were high and fast enough to get him home safe. He wished Stefan would line up his shot and hit it.

By the time the quartet was on the flat ground and halfway home, everything had changed. The clouds had chased themselves away and the disturbing wind had again turned and consumed itself until the air was still.

Donnie flew southwards along the first fairway before wheeling at the beach and heading back northwards along the adjacent eighteenth. She had to flap her wings in the stilling air, and as she passed the Rabbi she dipped the left and then the right.

It was a day of the unscheduled, thought Sebastian, but it's ending right.

"OK," said the Rabbi. "I believe. I believe in Donnie."

Brian couldn't believe the day kept turning out sunny and thought he might send another text to his Dublin cousin who hadn't been out for a visit. Brian was adapted to the wind and rain, and to assorted downturns in the fate cycle, but always happy when it turned out correctly. I'll take the five iron, he thought, I'm feeling grand. And I haven't had a single thought about a dead body since that terrorist. Or about teeth.

He saw Sebastian and the Rabbi respond to the wing-dip and regretted that he did not himself know much about the way of the pelican. There were pigeons in the old city and at Trinity, but not a pelican, and the River Liffey was shallow and putrid, and more likely you'd find a dead dog in it than a big, proud sea-going bird. Watched by the Rabbi, Brian guided his five iron through its gentle fade to the right, taking it past the left side bunkering and onto the fringe of the final green.

Stefan had not noticed the change in the weather because he was preoccupied. The day had been most unusual – a police siege, two rides in the helicopter, a challenging philosophical conversation with a psychopath, a violent death, a three club wind from several directions. One could not prepare for these things. His scorecard was all over the place. It had been scored by three different markers, whoever was not at the time engaged in a police siege. Miscellaneous writing styles, some by a doctor, hard to read, with smudging from the rain and with some big numbers. He wanted to finish well, and there remained a chance for B-grade. An eagle would do it.

The Rabbi had not, until now, known friendship with birds, but had again enjoyed his fellowship at Desolation Point. Sometimes the sense of belonging was so good it took him back to the terraces at Highbury where Arsenal played their home games in front of a tribe in which everybody belonged. The only discrimination these days was from within the Jewish congregation at the Central Synagogue, where some did not think he should play golf. After the sermon they gathered over the fish balls and talked about him. A golfing rabbi. He should be studying if he's not working, they said. After all, we are paying him.

As the foursome came on down towards their balls, the Rabbi was veering back towards anger over the congregation and their greed for all the fish balls. He was saved by the siren of an ambulance, which came from the west and swung onto the grass by the eighteenth green, disturbing the family of ducks. The siren was then turned off but the vehicle came straight at the Rabbi.

"What's going on?" he asked, and Sebastian replied, "That vehicle's upset Donnie. Look, she's flying north, away from the wretched noise. I don't like to finish the round without her."

The ambulance veered around the pair and continued south towards a group of golfers who appeared troubled by something on the ground.

Stefan stared and was thankful the ambulance was not for him. He hit with confidence from 150 metres. The ball took flight, soared, then bounced and rolled, and disappeared into the eighteenth hole. It was an eagle and he was a B-grader.

"I did it," he said, as a flight of black cockatoos took off and wheeled over the dunes.

"We knew you'd make it," said three golfers.

* * *

The final published result is blunt. There is no space on the scorecard for an explanation of what may have gone wrong. Or right. Just a number – the number of times the ball has been hit. Golfers do not require a theory, an excuse or a dissertation. The score would be read electronically, by a cold machine. Any love poetry included in the margins would lead to a response of *Unable to read score. Adjust and re-enter.*

Stefan was pleased as he signed his card. "It just doesn't tell the full story," he sighed. "I hit the ball well, until it all went wrong. And then I came back. I'll be in B-grade."

Sebastian signed his own card and focused on the near distance where the little wagtail who had accompanied him since the sixteenth tee now hopped off to join the following group. The ducks waddled and Donnie returned to her tower. *There would be a nominal winner,* he thought, and the winner would open the *Daily Telegraph* in the cafe to check his name, then buy a copy at the newsagency. The real story wasn't published, the story of ashes on the wind, a pelican who favoured a particular golfer, and the survival of souls exposed and tended patiently.

The real winner was Point Desolation herself, although some men achieved an honourable draw. Each had set out expecting to win, and this hope had been maintained for a time. In the end there was a pelican watching over four men who again held hands, performing the day's final sacrament.

Sebastian thanked his friends for their tenderness. "Until next time," he said.

"*Chaim*," said the Rabbi as usual, choosing the Hebrew word for life.

"Yes, life," said Sebastian. "It's bigger than the dream."

Stefan looked at him curiously.

"Indeed," said Brian, "life is what we've got."

With a lighter heart the Rabbi turned to face his work of honouring the dead. Stefan turned to face his future as a confident B-grader. Brian turned for the pub where he had a date with his old partner from the second row – a faithful relationship forged in the heat of the rugby scrum.

Sebastian met Donnie's gaze where she sat on her light tower, then turned for home, looking forward to seeing Magda. He felt again for the bracelet – *Not For Resuscitation*. Deftly, he removed it and slipped it into the rubbish bin by the eighteenth green, amidst the ripped scorecards, orange peel and apple cores. "I'll have that pacemaker," he said.

Donnie turned her bill, jumped, flapped and soared, straight towards the caves and the clever hermit.

* * *

I sat on my light tower and they came straight towards me, as always – always I'm there when they finish. They got through, there was no medical emergency, they looked happy. Sebastian looked at me. I was very tired but I'd done it.

Epilogue

When Donnie got back to the clever hermit, she saw that he had not moved on the couch. She watched and listened to his laboured breathing. She nudged him and he woke up.

The hermit spoke softly and Donnie leaned in close. "Well done, Donnie," he said, and coughed and then fought for breath. "He's got through again, hasn't he?"

Donnie laid her bill across Noel's lap and continued her watch.

Acknowledgments

Many thanks are due here.

First, there are pelicans (and other birds) at Long Reef Golf Links in Sydney. These birds have given me perspective. There are some plovers who migrate seasonally from Alaska, totally on course, while I cannot navigate the generous fairways but make regular trips sideways into the rough or over a cliff precipice. To be fair, these plovers get to a certain altitude, hitch onto an airstream and then get some sleep. I, however, never ever do that.

Then, there is a community of golfers at Long Reef. I have had connection and conversation to help me cope with what might otherwise have been a miserable journey. They have their quirks, these golfers, but Golf Interrupted is a work of fiction and does not carry truths within, for legal reasons.

Inside that other great universe of non-golfers, there are readers and writers who have done their best to pull me through and up. I did most of the raw writing in my writers' group, *Writestuff*, at the New South Wales Writers Centre. Paul Satchell read vignettes and suggested early sculpting. I workshopped scenes and chapters with the help of the masters program in Creative Writing at Macquarie University. Once a first draft came into being, it was critiqued and shaped by readers, Julie Anderson, Pete Anderson, Ruth Armstrong, Judith Daly, Marianne Hamilton, Margaret Mason, Jenny Murphy, Jo Strecker.

By the time the twelfth draft limped into the light, further debt had accrued, to Zoe Anderson, Kevin Barnes, Bill Blessing, Michael Diamond, Susan O'Brien, and again Julie Anderson. Workshopping continued in *Write to the End* at the New South Wales Writers Centre. Professional assistance and editing came from Carol Major, Varuna, Glenda Downing, Emily Maguire, and especially Stuart MacDonald. Publishing advice from Joel Naoum.

Most important, I thank my family for love and patience. Widows and orphans are for printers the bereft and lonely words left when sentences are cut by the page's ending, to leave a single word sitting on the page following. I am sure my family felt this way

– it is such long, arduous and solitary work to write a novel. And when I was with family I went on and on about golf and pelicans.